Emily Harvale lives in East Sussex, in the UK.
You can contact her via her website, Twitter, Facebook or
Pinterest

Author contacts:
www.emilyharvale.com
www.twitter.com/emilyharvale
www.facebook.com/emilyharvalewriter
www.facebook.com/emilyharvale
www.pinterest.com/emilyharvale

GW00630578

***

Scan the code above to see all Emily's books on Amazon

A Christmas Hideaway

Emily Harvale

ISBN 978-1-909917-12-5

Published by Crescent Gate Publishing

Print edition published worldwide 2015
E-edition published worldwide 2015

Editor Christina Harkness

Cover design by JR, Luke Brabants and Emily Harvale

Acknowledgements

My special thanks go to the following:

Christina Harkness for editing this novel. Christina has the patience of a saint and her input is truly appreciated.

My webmaster and friend, David Cleworth who does so much more for me than website stuff.

Luke Brabants and JR for their work on the gorgeous cover. JR is a genius in graphic design and Luke's a talented artist. Luke's website is: http://www.lukebrabants.com

My fabulous friends for their support and friendship.

My Twitter and Facebook friends, and fans of my Facebook author page. It's great to chat with you. You help to keep me (relatively) sane!

And finally, you – for buying this book. Thank You. It really means a lot to me. I hope you enjoy it.

This book is dedicated to Phoebe, my beloved cat who passed away in September. She was never: 'just a cat'. She was a friend and companion, a playmate and comforter, an excellent listener, never once passing judgement or criticizing my writing. After a long day, her soft snores were a delightful distraction and her loud, morning purrs were better than any alarm clock. She is greatly missed and will never be forgotten.
My desk isn't quite the same without you, curled up on it, Phoebe. xxx

Chapter One

Friday, 18th December

Holly Gilroy skidded across the tiled floor in her Santa-embellished slipper socks, pulled back the curtain and peered through her kitchen window into the ink-black sky of another bitterly cold, December evening. Something had clattered against the pane and she was anxious to see what it was.

'It's hailstones!'

She watched them smash against the window for a moment. Was the glass strong enough to cope with such an onslaught? On top of everything else, the last thing she needed right now was a broken window.

She was being ridiculous and she let the curtain fall, shutting out the storm.

If only she could shut out her memories with such ease.

She turned away, retrieved the large, ceramic bowl she'd dumped on the worktop and glanced at her sister, Ivy.

'It's hailstones,' she repeated. 'The size of frozen Brussels sprouts.'

Ivy was leaning on her elbows on the table in the centre of the kitchen, reading a hot-off-the-press edition of the Hideaway Down Village Newsletter. She grinned and raised her head, tossing a length of auburn hair over one shoulder.

'I've told you fifteen billion-trillion times. Don't exaggerate. Anyway, what did you think it was? A gang of hooligans throwing stones or something? Or maybe a group

1

of irate carollers foolish enough to venture out in this foul weather? It's been pouring since the minute I arrived.'

The Rayburn clonked, crackled and gurgled as it not only pumped another blast of heat to the radiators in Holly's Victorian cottage but also filled the air with the spicy aromas of a second batch of mince pies baking in one of its ovens. The first batch, complete with a heavy dusting of icing sugar, was cooling on two wire trays, side by side on one of the worktops. Holly stirred the gloopy, brandy-soaked mixed fruit in the bowl now cradled against her ribs, for a third batch.

'Of course not,' Holly said, trying not to meet her sister's eyes.

There was no way she was telling Ivy that for a split second she had thought it was Paul, doing what he'd done so many times during the fifteen years they had dated – even though she knew it wouldn't be him. The last time she'd seen him was over eleven months ago. Eleven months, seventeen days and – she glanced at the cat-shaped wall clock – eighteen hours, give or take a couple of minutes.

Having left in unpleasant circumstances, the last thing he'd be doing was throwing gravel at her window at six o'clock on the final Friday evening before Christmas Day, so yes, for a nanosecond, she'd thought it might be hooligans.

Then she'd realised that was equally unlikely. There were no hooligans in Hideaway Down. There were hardly any people. It had a population of a mere two hundred and thirty-nine and most of those wouldn't make it up the steep hill leading from the village to the top of Hideaway Cliff, where, at one end of a row of four, her red-brick cottage stood.

It was usually festooned with multi-coloured, twinkling

lights at this time of year but other than a holly wreath hanging on the dark-green front door, Holly had made no attempt to welcome in the festive season. A circumstance which, Ivy had informed Holly the moment she had arrived: "... we're going to do something about, this weekend."

Of those who would make it up Hideaway Hill to the cliff top, only twenty were between the ages of five and thirty and none of those leant towards vandalism. Well, perhaps one or two of the five-year-olds showed a natural ability to break things, but that was simply due to childish enthusiasm, not to malice aforethought.

Paul was the only person Holly had ever known to throw stones at her window – and that was more of a tradition than either a need to attract her attention, or bad behaviour on his part. And he was thirty-one this year. Not that his age had anything to do with the matter.

Why did every single thought that popped into her head have to revolve around Paul Best? Couldn't she get through at least one day without thinking about him?

She was determined to think of something else, even if it was something equally depressing.

'Can you hear the sea crashing against the cliff?'

'Yeah.' Ivy pushed back her chair, reached the kitchen worktop in just three steps and switched on the kettle. 'I wouldn't be surprised if we lose another sliver of cliff if this wet weather continues.'

'One day I'll wake up and this cottage, along with the others of course, will be on the beach. Mum will have to rent them out as seaside cottages – literally – not "cliff-top cottages with unrivalled three hundred and sixty degree views of the sea; a quaint English village and countryside designated as an Area of Outstanding Natural Beauty".'

Holly was only half-joking. Every long tide or severe

3

storm chipped away more of the chalk clay cliff. Jarvis Pope, head of the Hideaway Cliff Preservation Trust, regularly took measurements to record the amount of erosion, and every year at least a metre and sometimes several metres, crumbled into the sea. That may not seem a lot but when Holly's maternal grandparents bought the cottages they were more than two thousand metres from the ragged edge of the cliff. Now they were one thousand and ten; probably less by tomorrow. That was a lot of ground to lose in fifty years.

'It's definitely a dark and stormy night,' Ivy said, grinning and clearly attempting to lighten the mood. 'I'm so glad my boss told me I could leave early today. It was still sunny in London when I left this afternoon and the drive down was great. Wouldn't fancy doing it in this weather. Want a cup of tea?' She waved a Christmas-themed mug in front of Holly's face.

'I'd rather have a glass of wine.'

Holly switched on the radio, blocking out the sound of the waves battering the cliff and the hailstones pounding the windows. She must shake off this sense of melancholy. It was the season to be jolly, after all. She managed a smile as Ivy sang along to *Santa Claus is Coming to Town*.

Ivy grabbed a bottle of red wine from the rack, poured a large glass for Holly and popped a teabag in the Christmassy mug. She handed Holly the glass and leant against the worktop.

'It said in the newsletter they're taking bets again on who'll win the 'Best Mince Pie' contest this year. You should enter. Your mince pies are to die for.'

She reached out and took one from the cooling tray, sinking her teeth into the melt-in-the-mouth, shortcrust pastry, with a loud, satisfied sigh. A scattering of icing sugar floated down and landed on her cashmere sweater.

4

'There's no point. Petunia's won it every year for the past twenty years or so. Mum reckons it's rigged but the plain fact is, Petunia's mince pies are as close to perfection as it's possible for a mince pie to be.'

'That's true. But there may be something in what Mum says. Petunia's mince pies aren't the only thing close to perfection as far as old Bartram's concerned. And he has the deciding vote.'

Holly grinned. Bartram Battersfold, the village butcher, had a bit of a crush on Petunia Welsley, there was no denying that – although he did deny it if anyone mentioned it. Petunia seemed blissfully unaware of his armour, or his rheumy eyes watching her every move, or that he puffed out his red cheeks and licked his lips whenever she spoke to him but then Petunia seemed blissfully unaware of most things. She had wafted around the village in a heavenly-smelling, invisible cloud for as long as Holly could remember. It was as if she lived in her own little world of scented oils and herbs, the ingredients with which she worked. People came from miles around to buy soaps, shampoos, perfumes and other delights from Petunia's Perfumery. And Bartram was probably the best-smelling, fifty-year-old butcher in the south of England.

'I also read that the Christmas Market's still going ahead on Sunday,' Ivy continued. 'But when I drove past Market Field this afternoon, it looked more like quagmire than a field. The village pond's on the verge of overflowing too. Shoppers will have to wear those all-in-one boots and trousers, Gramps wears when he goes fishing at Hideaway Hole. Or go around the stalls in little boats. Ooh! Punters, punting. That might catch on.'

'Kev the Rev offered the church hall if the bad weather continued and as it's done nothing but rain… or hail for weeks now, I think we can say with some certainty, it'll be in the church hall.'

'That's a shame. I quite like the idea of a floating market. It still makes me laugh to think of our new vicar wearing a T-shirt with 'Kev the Rev' scrawled across the front. Especially as his name's Burt.'

'No it's not. His name's Kevin. Kevin Longbourne... oh, you were joking. I think it's cool. And it gives the oldies something else to moan about.'

'That's true. In other news, it said preparations for The Snowdrop Bash are ahead of schedule. But you already know that because you're helping Mum organise it this year, aren't you?'

'I help organise it every year,' Holly said. 'But I'm usually working so can only help out in my free time. This December, I've had a lot of free time. Plus Kev the Rev's been helping, so we've had an extra pair of hands.'

'He's really throwing himself into village life, isn't he? Gramps told me the man's constantly racing around, poking his nose into everything. Perhaps his T-shirt should say: Revved-up, Kev, or Kev the Rev Racer.'

'Gramps shouldn't be saying unpleasant things about the Reverend, and you shouldn't be making jokes about him. Although he'd probably be the first one to laugh. He's got a good sense of humour and he's a breath of fresh air after the last vicar.'

'That's also true. That one's T-shirt would have said: Vincent the Venomous Vicar.'

Holly laughed at that. Ivy always made Holly feel better. Although they were twins and looked similar, they weren't identical, either in looks or personalities. Ivy was more of an extrovert than Holly and definitely the prettier, in Holly's opinion. And Ivy loved change and excitement – which is why she'd moved up to London, whereas Holly preferred things to stay the same and loved living in

Hideaway Down. Or at least she had.

Ivy made her tea and took another mince pie. 'Don't scowl at me. I need sustenance if I'm working at the pub all night. Plus I've got to get there in this bloody awful weather, so I deserve a treat or two. You owe me big time.'

There was no denying that. Ivy hadn't hesitated when Holly had Skyped her at the beginning of the week and told her the latest, dreadful news: that Paul was returning to Hideaway Down for Christmas... and he was bringing Naomi with him.

'I can't possibly help Mum in the pub!' Holly had shrieked, tears streaming down her cheeks. 'I can't face him, Ivy. I can't face seeing them together. I'd rather die! I'll have to go away somewhere for Christmas. I can't stay here.'

'Calm down,' Ivy had replied. 'There's no point in making rash decisions and there's no way that jerk, Paul or that cow, Naomi are going to ruin this family's Christmas. Look, I've got some holiday to spare. I was coming down on the 23rd anyway. I'll just tell my boss I need to go home for a family emergency. He's the best boss in the world, so there won't be a problem. I'll come down this Friday instead and I'll take over your pub duties.'

'You'll do that for me?' Holly wasn't really surprised.

'Yes. And you can even hide away in your cottage for some of the time so that you don't bump into them.'

'You're my saviour. The best sister in the whole wide world. Thank you! I'll buy you something spectacular for Christmas.'

'No you won't!' Ivy said. 'Don't you dare waste your redundancy money on Christmas presents. That's for your future. Just remember me when you win the lottery, or marry a millionaire or something.'

'It's a deal.'

'But you've got to promise me that, no matter what, you'll still come to The Snowdrop Bash. You're a Gilroy. You've got to be there. The Gilroys have organised The Snowdrop Bash for more than fifty years. It's our Christmas party and you're not going to let me, Mum and Gramps down, and that's an end to that discussion. I'll see you on Friday. In the meantime, don't start panicking about the situation, okay?'

'Okay,' Holly had agreed, knowing she'd be doing nothing other than panic about it.

She hadn't seen her ex-boyfriend, Paul – or her ex-best friend, Naomi – since they'd done a disappearing act together last New Year's Eve, and the thought of the pair of them being all lovey-dovey in The Snowdrop Inn was more than Holly's broken heart could bear. Her mum had said there was no way she was letting Paul Best or Naomi Evans put one foot inside the door of her pub but Holly wasn't taking any chances.

As for going to The Snowdrop Bash – that was a definite no-no. It annoyed her immensely that she wouldn't be able to go to something she'd attended every year since she was old enough to walk, but she couldn't face it. She couldn't walk into The Snowdrop Inn on Christmas Eve without Paul by her side. She'd have to say she'd got the flu or something and sit at home alone. But she wouldn't tell Ivy that either. It might be the Gilroy's annual Christmas party but what was the point in going to a party if you didn't want to be there? That would only ruin it for everyone else. There was no way she'd do that.

'Earth to Holly.' Ivy clicked her fingers in front of Holly's face.

'Sorry. I was miles away. You're right. I do owe you.'

'I was joking, Holly. You don't owe me a thing. You'd do the same for me and you know I prefer working in the pub to looking after the guests at these cottages any day of the week, so you're actually doing me the favour. Mum would've roped me in to help out, as she does every year. Still, at least she pays us, so it's not slave labour.'

'You'd do it for free and so would I. But this year, the money will really come in handy. I've got to be sensible, I know. My redundancy was quite good, all things considered but it won't go far if I can't find another job in the New Year.'

'You'll find something. And you can always move up to London and live with me. There's nothing to... I mean, there's no reason why you can't, now you're no longer working in Eastbourne. Anyway, there's plenty of time to think about that. We can chat about it over Christmas and for now, you've got the job of head chef and bottle washer at Gilroy's Happy Holiday Cottages and I've got a second job of assistant barmaid at The Snowdrop Inn.'

Holly knew what her sister really meant. There was nothing to keep her in Hideaway Down. She'd lost her long-term boyfriend last year, as well as her best friend, and this year she'd lost the job she and Paul used to argue about so often; the job she loved almost as much as she loved him. The job she thought she'd have for life – Manager of Turning Pages, the latest incarnation of one of the oldest, independent book shops in Eastbourne... until Ralph Turner, the owner had decided it was no longer viable and closed the doors at the end of November. Holly had worked there since leaving university with an English Literature degree and a life-long passion for books and she had no idea what she would – or could – do now. Thirty-one wasn't old but it was a bit late to be starting out on a new career path.

Ivy snaffled a third mince pie. 'What time are the first lot of guests arriving? I hope they can find their way in this

9

weather. It's hard enough to find the village or these cottages in broad daylight, so…' Her voice trailed off as she brushed specs of icing sugar from the front of her sweater.

'I'm not really sure when they're arriving. I think one's supposed to be arriving tonight. He's an author apparently but I've never heard of him. Gabriel… something or other. The rest are coming tomorrow. Mum sent detailed maps and you know what she's like with her directions. Every bump in the road will be marked and every turning highlighted with precise distances and appropriate speeds, so getting here shouldn't be a problem. Apart from the weather.'

Ivy grinned. 'You've gotta love Mum and her maps. An author, eh? At least you'll have something to talk about. How old is he?'

'No idea.'

Holly opened the fridge door and took out a ball of pastry she'd made earlier, sprinkled a section of the worktop with flour, removed the cling film from the pastry and grabbed her rolling pin.

'Er. Exactly how many guests are you expecting? Didn't Mum say you only had to give them each a cup of tea and a mince pie when they come to collect the keys and then send them on their merry ways to their respective cottages? I think seventy-two mince pies might be overdoing it.'

Holly tutted. 'Sixty-nine now you've eaten three. They're not just for this evening and tomorrow. They'll keep for some time, especially with the amount of brandy I've added to the mincemeat. It'll save me making them fresh each day for afternoon tea. I'm expecting seven guests. Or is it eight?'

'Don't ask me. You're the one being paid to take care of them.'

'Yeah. My future's certainly looking bright, isn't it?'

'C'mon Holly. Don't get all maudlin again. It's nearly Christmas. And we love Christmas, remember? It's full of festive fun, fun, fun.'

'I did love it. Now I'm dreading it. It's my first Christmas without him.'

'But that doesn't mean it's going to be awful. This could be the best Christmas ever. The one where all your dreams come true. The one you'll be telling your great-great-granddaughters about when you're one hundred and one years old.'

'Yeah. The one where I got made redundant. The one where, when I went into Maisy Miller's Bakery for a comforting, freshly baked doughnut, she asked me what I thought about Paul bringing his 'new' girlfriend home for the holidays. The one where I hide away and cook and clean for the guests at the cottages over Christmas and New Year whilst everyone tells me to "keep my spirits up". The one—'

'Okay! I get the picture. Things are bad for you at the moment. But being miserable isn't going to make things better, Holly. In fact if anything, it'll make things worse.'

Holly thumped the rolling pin onto the pastry and grabbed her glass. In her haste, a few drops of wine spilt over the rim and landed in the centre of the large, white snowflake on the front of her red, wool sweater.

Ivy tore off a piece of kitchen towel covered with pictures of elves.

'Santa's little helpers,' she said, handing it to Holly with a feeble smile.

'Thanks. I was about to say things couldn't get much worse. But it seems they can.'

11

Chapter Two

Gabriel Hardwick slammed on his brakes and cursed several times. Could things get any worse? He peered into the darkness through the barrage of hailstones. Where the hell was he?

He was certain he'd seen this crossroads before but he'd seen so many crossroads in the last half hour that it was possible he was driving round in circles. This one had an almost identical sign to the last one except this one 'informed' him that Hideaway Down was three miles back in the direction he'd just come and the previous one had pointed him three miles in this direction.

Bryony was right. He was a stupid, arrogant dick for thinking he could just drive off and spend Christmas alone in some tiny cliff-top cottage hideaway. At this rate he'd still be looking for the bloody place on New Year's Eve.

Spending the holidays at a rented cottage overlooking the sea in one direction and countryside and villages in the other, had seemed like a brilliant plan when he'd booked it two months ago. He wasn't looking forward to Christmas this year and ignoring it was the best way to get through it. He'd be able to finish his new novel; take long walks on the beach; tramp over the hills or through the woods. He'd lounge in a comfy armchair strategically positioned in front of a roaring log fire, a book in one hand, a large glass of red wine in the other. He'd have time to think, time to relax and time to plan his future.

Now, stuck in the middle of nowhere, the plan had lost a

great deal of its sparkle.

The directions kindly sent to him by Mrs Janet Gilroy, the friendly woman from whom he was renting the cottage, had told him that he would reach Ivy Cottage in one hour and fifty-five minutes from his home in Surrey. That was on the basis that he adhered to the relevant speed limits, which she'd also marked, where appropriate, together with each and every turning and road sign, along with two sets of road works which she'd said might cause a short delay. She had helpfully mentioned that it may take longer in bad weather but what she had neglected to tell him was that her directions were bloody useless in the dark and that one country lane and crossroad looked very much like another when you had no idea where you were going and couldn't see a thing through the chunks of ice pounding your windscreen. Weren't there any street lights in this county?

His satnav was equally confused. It contradicted Janet Gilroy's directions at every turn. He'd been driving for almost three hours and the thing was sounding as stressed and annoyed as he was. It had just informed him that he was five miles from his destination. The crossroad's sign said three, although he clearly couldn't trust that.

This had turned into a bloody awful day. He'd intended a leisurely afternoon drive through the Surrey and Sussex countryside which would look resplendent on such a cold but sunny winter's day. Unfortunately, he'd misplaced his laptop charger and then his glasses and by the time he'd found them, rain was bouncing off his driveway and Bryony was on his doorstep, intent on thwarting his plans.

Bryony had a knack for doing that: thwarting his plans. That was one of the reasons he'd ended their relationship two months ago – although not the main reason – and it was only their personal relationship he'd ended. Their business relationship of author and agent was still ongoing.

Despite Bryony being a little crazy as far as Gabriel's personal life was concerned, she was nothing but professional regarding his writing career. She was a damned good agent too. He'd hate for them to part company completely.

But today had been personal and she'd turned up unannounced. Having to tell her yet again that no, he hadn't changed his mind and no, he didn't want to spend the holidays with her, wasn't his idea of fun. Agreeing that yes, he did miss having sex with her was a big mistake. Stopping her from stripping naked and from ripping his clothes off for "one last romp between the sheets for old time's sake… and because it's Christmas", had come close to an all-out battle – and one he'd been in danger of losing. God, that woman was determined.

He'd finally managed to make her see sense… or he thought he had. Suddenly, she'd burst into tears and if there was one thing he hated it was seeing a woman cry. Comforting her had clearly given her mixed signals and eventually, some three hours after he'd originally planned to leave, he decided he had no choice. He left her the spare keys to his house, told her to let herself out whenever she was ready and legged it to his car; swear words and threats trailing after him like a string of broken fairy lights.

Would he return in the New Year to find the place trashed? He'd read about women who did that. But Bryony wasn't that kind of woman… was she? They'd dated for almost two years but sometimes he had felt she was a complete stranger and he didn't know her at all. Especially when she made her threats.

'I could make your world come crashing down around you, Mr Gabriel Hardwick,' she had spat at him when he had ended their relationship. 'Don't forget you need me.'

How could he forget? She had reminded him several

times since then, including twice today.

He had forgotten his umbrella though, but there was no way he was going back for it. So between his front door and his car, he'd got soaked and instead of leaving in daylight, he'd driven off in the dark and the rain.

What a fabulous start to his Christmas holidays!

Now he was lost in the middle of nowhere, in the worst hailstorm he'd ever seen and on top of that, his iPhone battery had died.

He was tired. Tired and pissed off. He shut his eyes and let his head fall back against the headrest. Where and when had he last seen any signs of civilisation? If he could get to a house, a pub or a shop, he could get his bearings. Either that or he could borrow a phone and call the helpful Janet Gilroy for additional directions. He couldn't be that far away now. It was either three miles or five, if either the crossroads or the satnav were to be believed.

A screech of tyres and the blaring of a horn made his heart thud against his chest. His eyes shot open to find the front of a large, mud-covered tractor inches away from the shiny, red bonnet of his car.

An irate-looking tractor-driver was shouting and waving at him but he couldn't hear a word over the sound of the hail and, having been saturated once today, there was no way he was getting out of his car in this weather. The other man had no such qualms. He plonked a flat, tweed cap on his bush of ginger hair, jumped down from his seat and marched towards Gabriel.

Gabriel opened the window a fraction.

'You can't park here!' the man said, towering above the window. 'It's a busy road. You're bloody lucky I didn't crash right into you.'

Busy road? Gabriel hadn't seen another vehicle for over an hour... until now and this narrow, pothole-ridden lane wasn't his idea of a road, busy or otherwise.

'I'm sorry,' he said. 'I'm lost. I'm looking for Hideaway Down. Gilroy's Happy Holiday Cottages, to be precise. Have you heard of them?'

The man brightened. 'Of course I have. Everyone hereabouts knows the Gilroys. How come you're lost then? All you need do is follow the signs.' He pointed at the crossroads' sign.

If only it were that simple.

'Er. I did. One said three miles this way. That one says three miles back there.' He pointed over his shoulder. 'They can't both be right.'

The man nodded. 'They are.'

If this was some kind of intelligence test, Gabriel had clearly failed. He shook his head and laughed, although he wasn't finding the situation funny.

'They can't be.'

The man drew large, work-worn hands onto his hips and puffed out his cheeks. He seemed oblivious to the hailstones bouncing off his shoulders but as he was built like a barn, he probably didn't feel them.

'You calling me a liar?'

'No! I'm merely saying that if two signs are pointing in different directions but purporting to be leading to the same place, one of them must be wrong.'

'Oh you are, are you? Well, if you know so much, it's a mystery why you're lost and that's a fact.' He bent down and peered through the window. 'That's your problem.' He pointed a sausage-like finger at the satnav. 'What you need to do is take no notice of that and follow the signs instead. They're as plain as day.'

Gabriel sighed. The only signs "as plain as day" were the signs that he had left civilisation far behind and had arrived in some backwater hell.

16

'Forgive me,' he said. 'I'm not from around here so perhaps I'm not reading the signs in the same way as local people. Could you possibly just point me in the right direction, please? Or to the nearest phone. I don't want to keep you chatting in this foul weather.'

The man frowned and rubbed his chin before pointing to Gabriel's iPhone on the passenger seat. 'That's your nearest phone.'

Gabriel sucked in a breath. 'Yes. Thank you. The battery's dead, unfortunately.'

'Nearest one's in The Snowdrop Inn then.'

'Perhaps you would be kind enough to tell me how to get to The Snowdrop Inn, please?'

The man stood upright. 'It's in Hideaway Down. Just follow the signs,' he said, pointing to the crossroad's sign as he turned and walked away.

This was bloody ridiculous. Gabriel grabbed his coat from the passenger seat and threw it over his shoulders. He shoved the car door open and ran after the man.

'Look,' Gabriel said, stepping in front of him. 'Perhaps I'm stupid. I know I'm exhausted. It's been a shitty day and now I'm saturated. All I want is to find Ivy Cottage. Or Hideaway Down. Or Janet Gilroy. Or this… Snowdrop Inn. If you'll show me the way to any of those, I'll make it worth your while.'

The man's eyes narrowed and a broad but oddly creepy smile spread across his weather-beaten features. Gabriel noticed the man's two front teeth were missing. A momentary flash of several horror films rolled into one flickered before Gabriel's eyes but surely that was merely his writer's imagination working overtime?

'How much?' the man asked.

'Fifty quid.' Gabriel said it without hesitation. Fifty pounds seemed like a pittance in exchange for a hot bath

17

and a warm bed but from the expression on this stranger's face, it seemed like a Christmas miracle.

'Fifty quid! You having me on? Fifty quid just to take you three miles?'

So the crossroads hadn't told a complete lie; his satnav had. Gabriel nodded. 'Yep. And I'll give you half now and half when we get there.'

The man reached out an arm and for a second, Gabriel had a rush of adrenaline. The man could mug him right here. Instead, he grabbed Gabriel by the arm and led him back to his car.

'Best get out of the road then. Don't want to get run over. Got yourself a deal. You follow me. I was going for a pint in The Snowdrop Inn anyway but I'll take you to the foot of Hideaway Hill. You can see Ivy Cottage from there, up on Hideaway Cliff.'

Gabriel pulled his wallet from his coat pocket and went to pay the man. A huge, paddle-like hand stopped him.

'You keep your money. It's Christmas and the season of goodwill. If you're staying in Hideaway Down you can buy me a pint in The Snowdrop Inn sometime. I'm in there every evening. We're going that way so you need to turn your car around.'

Great. Back in the direction he'd just driven.

Gabriel made a three-point turn at the crossroads and followed the man and his tractor at a snail's pace. At this rate, it would be midnight before they covered the three miles but he was curious to see how both the crossroads' signs could be correct, as his guide had assured him they were.

About one mile back along the road, he saw the tractor indicate to turn right. Was he going to drive through that massive hedge? Oh shit! Was the guy taking him across fields or something?

18

But wait. There was a gap in the hedge. Actually... it was more than a gap. It was a turning. A turning from one lane into another lane. A lane which Gabriel had driven past at least three times, if not more, without even spotting it. And now he also saw the sign, half-covered by the overgrown, evergreen hedge. It read: Hideaway Lane. Hideaway Down: 2 miles. So both of the crossroads had been right. The turning for Hideaway Lane was midway between both signs and from there it was two miles further on. He remembered seeing a turning on the map he'd been sent but he couldn't see the real thing for the trees and hedges and the torrential rain and hail.

He crawled along in second gear behind the tractor. Life really was simple when you knew where you were going. Or when you had someone to show you the way.

Chapter Three

Holly was brushing her teeth when the doorbell rang. She dashed downstairs in her dancing reindeer-pattered pyjamas and flung the door open. She was expecting to see Ivy who'd just texted her to say she was about to leave the pub and she had some news. Why Ivy had rung the doorbell was a mystery; Holly had given her the spare key.

'Did you use Santa's magic dust? That was... Oh! You're not my sister, Ivy.'

Dark, questioning eyes met hers. They reminded her of Irish coffee – without the cream. Even darker brows drew together in an irritated frown and droplets of water dripped from expresso-coffee-coloured hair onto broad shoulders covered by an expensive-looking, navy-blue coat.

The hail had stopped but an icy wind suddenly hit her and goosebumps prickled around her body like a real-life dot-to-dot. The dark eyes flickered over her and the frown deepened.

'I'm Gabriel Hardwick. I'm renting Ivy Cottage. Janet Gilroy told me to collect the keys from Holly Cottage. This is Holly Cottage, isn't it? The sign on the door says it is but I'm a bit wary of signs today. I apologise for my late arrival. I got lost.'

His voice *was* the cream. Smooth, rich and sexy with an edginess bordering on impatience, but Holly couldn't stop shivering.

'It's freezing!' She ran along the tiny hall, expecting him to follow but when she glanced back, the only thing following her was a strange look in his eyes. 'Well, come in

20

then. And shut the door. I'll get the keys. I thought Mum sent you a map. Didn't you use it?'

He hesitated, glanced towards Ivy Cottage as if in two minds before stepping into the hall and closing the door. 'Mum? Oh, of course. You're Janet Gilroy's daughter. Sorry, I can't recall your name. Yes, I did try to use the map but in the dark and the storm, I missed the turn-off for the village. I can see why it's called Hideaway Down. It's very well hidden. A local farmer eventually came to my rescue and showed me the way here.'

'I'm Holly. The keys are in here.' She went into the kitchen and this time he did follow her. 'Would you like a cup of tea and a mince pie?' She filled the kettle and switched it on. 'Did he have bushy ginger hair?'

'Sorry? What? The farmer, you mean? Yes, he did and no to the tea and mince pie. Er. Thanks. Look, I don't mean to be rude but do you have the keys, please? It's been a very long drive and I'm knack… exhausted.'

'There're homemade and most people think they're delicious.'

'What are? Oh, the mince pies. I'm sure they are. I just want to go to bed. Maybe tomorrow.'

'Take some with you.'

Holly handed him a tin with the Twelve Days of Christmas depicted round the edges. She'd placed six mince pies in it earlier. He looked at it as if he wasn't sure what to do with it.

'Thanks. The keys?'

From a rack containing four sets of keys, Holly took the set with a tag bearing a beautifully painted picture of a sprig of ivy and handed it to him.

'You'll find a welcome pack on the kitchen worktop and there's milk in the fridge. It's delivered fresh every day from the local dairy, so you'll get more in the morning. If

21

there's anything you need, just come and ring my bell. Are you sure you don't want a cup of tea? You look a bit… damp.'

'I got soaked asking for directions. All I want is a hot shower and a comfy bed. Good night… Holly, wasn't it? Sorry, I'm dreadful with names. I can't even recall the name of the farmer I met tonight. Or perhaps he didn't tell me. I'm not making any sense. I need to go to sleep. Goodnight. And thanks.' He turned to leave.

'It was probably Henry. Henry Goode. He owns Hideaway Farm.'

He glanced back. 'He didn't tell me then. I'd have remembered the name Henry. That's my dad's name. I expect the farm's well hidden too.'

'The farm? No, you can see it from here. Well, not this time of night obviously but in the morning you'll see it. Most of it. There're five hundred acres surrounding the village and spreading across several hills in the distance. These cottages used to be part of it until my grandparents bought them fifty years ago.'

'Fascinating. I really need to get some sleep. Goodnight.'

'Oh. Goodnight then. Don't let the bedbugs bite.'

He stopped in his tracks. 'Bedbugs?'

Holly laughed at the horrified expression on his face – which was actually rather handsome if you liked dark-haired, dark-eyed men. She preferred fair-haired men… like Paul.

'It's just a saying. There aren't any bedbugs, don't worry. Perhaps I should've said: Pleasant dreams.'

'I think it's too late for that. Bedbugs. Yuk.' He shook, visibly.

She shouldn't have mentioned bedbugs. He seemed to have taken her seriously.

'Trust me. You'll sleep like a baby and I promise you, you won't find any kind of bugs, bed or otherwise in Ivy Cottage. I cleaned it within an inch of its life today. The place positively gleams.'

He gave her a wane smile. 'Goodnight,' he said, closing the front door.

It was only when she went back into the kitchen that she saw the tin of mince pies on the table. She ran along the hall and yanked open the door.

'You forgot these,' she called after him, a blast of icy air slapping her across the face.

'No I didn't.'

As he walked up the path to Ivy Cottage he appeared to be trying not to look in her direction, which, seeing that Ivy Cottage was next door to hers, was a bit difficult.

'Don't you want them?' Holly asked, peering round her doorframe when he reached up to put the key in the lock of his door. 'You might fancy one later.'

He glanced across at her. 'Thanks. But I won't.' He shoved the door open, stepped inside and closed it promptly.

Despite the ice-cold air creeping under her pyjamas, Holly stood on the doorstep, staring at the dark blue door of Ivy Cottage, its wreath of ivy and clove-studded oranges swaying in the wind.

'Who was that?' Ivy asked, trotting up the path as Holly was about to close her own door. 'Was it the author-guy?'

'I didn't hear you arrive,' Holly said, stepping back into the hall. 'Yes. His name's Gabriel. He's a bit... brusque.'

'Nice form though. Although the coat hid most of him. How old?'

'Mid-thirties I would guess. What?' Ivy was grinning at her.

'Did you open the door looking like that?' She stepped

inside and closed the door.

'Oh God! I should've put a dressing gown on. You can't see through them, can you?'

Ivy shrugged off her coat and laughed. 'That's the least of your worries. Look in the mirror.'

Holly glanced at her reflection in the large oval mirror in the hall.

Oh. My. God!

There was a ring of white toothpaste encircling her mouth and she'd completely forgotten that she'd wound a long length of red and gold Christmas ribbon around her scrunched-up, thick, auburn hair and tied it with a large bow before she'd started baking that afternoon. Ivy had laughed about it when she'd arrived. Holly was going to untie it before she went to bed.

'What must the guy have thought? A grown woman wearing dancing reindeer PJs, her hair piled high like some weird Christmas present on her head and a ring of toothpaste round her mouth.'

'At least you made a memorable first impression. And we all know how important first impressions are.'

Ivy was still laughing as she strolled into the kitchen.

No wonder the guy had been in such a hurry to get away and no wonder he didn't want the mince pies. She looked demented. And on top of that, she had to go and mention bedbugs.

Chapter Four

Saturday, 19th December

Gabriel opened his eyes and glanced around the room. For a moment, he'd forgotten where he was. He'd slept much better than he'd expected and although he would have preferred a quick shower, last night's bath had definitely improved his mood. As had meeting Holly Gilroy. He smiled at the memory. Should he have told her she had toothpaste round her mouth? Either she had no idea or she didn't care. And that hairdo. What was that about? Did she go out looking like a crazy person?

Then there were those pyjamas. The last time he'd seen PJs like that was on his eight-year-old niece. He didn't have a clue how old Holly was but she was considerably older than eight. Late twenties, early thirties he would guess.

But she was prettier than he'd imagined, in spite of all that. Not that he'd given her much thought when Janet Gilroy's directions had instructed him to "collect the keys from my daughter at Holly Cottage, the cottage with the green door, to your right as you approach the row of four".

There was something about her though. There must have been. He'd had a dream involving her and, whilst he couldn't recall it in its entirety, he could remember bits and pieces and the recollection made his smile grow wider.

He threw back the duvet and the red and white Christmas fleece on top of it and got up. He shivered. It was much colder this morning. In fact, it was freezing. He marched up to the radiator and touched it. Virtually stone cold. Great. He glanced at his watch. Six a.m. What time did the heating come on? Had he read anything about that in the details sent to him? He'd been so tired last night that he hadn't read the welcome pack. He'd just poured himself a glass of red from one of the several bottles he'd brought with him, soaked away his bad mood in the cast iron bath, and gone to bed. The radiators were working last night and it must have been midnight, if not later, by the time he finally went to sleep in a warm and cosy, albeit rather 'twee' bedroom.

Throwing on his dressing gown, he rushed downstairs, almost tumbling due to their steep angle. In the kitchen, which was slightly warmer than his bedroom, sat the unopened welcome pack and a box of groceries. He filled up the kettle, switched it on and grabbed the pack, flicking quickly through it.

All he could see were instructions about the Rayburn. No point in reading those right now. That was the cooker. He'd spotted it last night when he came in for a wine glass. The only other instructions seemed to be how to light and maintain a fire in the wood burner. Even he knew roughly how to do that, so he skipped those. Nothing about the central heating that he could see.

He glanced around the kitchen. He couldn't see a boiler. That was odd. There were radiators so there must be a boiler. All he had to do was locate it, or find the thermostat and set it to a higher temperature. How difficult could that be?

After twenty minutes he gave up searching, threw some logs in the wood burner, lit it with the firelighters provided and ran upstairs to get dressed, shivering as he did so. By the time he came back down a few tiny flames flickered against the logs but they were nowhere near enough to keep him warm. He had three choices. He could sit here and

26

wrap himself in blankets – assuming he could find some – go back to bed and hope the heating would come on, or go next door and see if Holly was up yet.

He decided on the latter and a few moments later he was standing at the door of Holly Cottage. It was now six-thirty and still dark but he could see a light in the upstairs window. Holly was awake although she may not be up. He hesitated before ringing the bell. What was the worst that could happen? She could ignore him or tell him to come back later but he was a paying guest and she had told him to ring her bell if he needed anything. Well, he needed heat.

He pressed the bell and rubbed his bare hands together in a vain attempt to get warm as he waited. It suddenly occurred to him that Holly had the same name as the cottage in which she lived. And hadn't she mentioned a sister last night called Ivy? Or had he imagined that? It was like the chicken and the egg. Which had come first? The cottages or the sisters' names? He smiled in spite of the fact he was freezing to death.

A sudden burst of heat hit him as Holly opened the door, still wearing those PJs and oddly enough, holding a toothbrush in her hand. This time there wasn't a ring of white around her mouth but there was a tiny trickle from the left side of it. She may be a bit crazy but at least she took her oral hygiene seriously.

'Morning Harry. Oh! I thought you were Harry with the milk.'

She looked as surprised to see him this morning as she had last night but there was something different about her today. The hair. This morning it tumbled over her shoulders, lustrous in the light from the hall.

'Harry? No, it's me. Gabriel. The guy who's renting Ivy Cottage.'

She frowned. 'I know who you are. I just thought you

27

were someone else. I wasn't expecting you.'

'You told me to come to you if I needed anything.'

'And you need something already? Sorry, that didn't come out right.'

'I'm so sorry to be a nuisance, but I'm an early riser and...' The trickle was about to drop onto her pyjama top. He reached out to wipe it away.

She stepped back, glaring at him and holding the toothbrush in front of her as if it were some sort of sword. He couldn't help but laugh.

'I was just going to... um... you have a trickle of toothpaste running down your chin. I was going to wipe it away.'

She looked even more horrified and her free hand shot to her mouth.

'Other side,' Gabriel added.

She stuck out her tongue and licked at the toothpaste and a sudden burst of warmth pumped through Gabriel's veins. Was he getting turned on by a woman dribbling toothpaste and wearing dancing reindeer PJs? God forbid.

He needed to think of something else... fast.

'That looks like it could so some serious damage,' he quipped, nodding his head towards the toothbrush which she still held aloft in her other hand.

'Huh? Oh. This is harmless,' she said, her cheeks turning a delightful shade of red as she smiled at him, her green eyes half-hidden by long, dark lashes.

But as she hurriedly lowered it, a bead of toothpaste shot off the end and landed on his cashmere coat, like paint flicked from an artist's brush. Except there was nothing artistic about the long white streak seeping into his breast pocket. How could such a tiny amount cover such a large area?

'Not so harmless after all,' he said, pulling a

28

handkerchief from his pocket and dabbing at the offending stain.

'I'm so sorry!' Holly shrieked. 'I didn't mean to do that. I didn't do it on purpose.'

'I didn't think you did. Don't worry about it.'

'I'll… I'll pay for the cleaning.'

He met her eyes. 'It's not a problem. Forget it.'

'Come into the kitchen. I may have something that'll remove it.'

'Honestly, don't worry.' There was no way he was letting her near his coat. She'd probably do more damage. 'The reason I'm here is because the heating in my cottage doesn't seem to be working. The radiators are virtually stone cold and I couldn't find anything to turn the temperature up.'

'Really? Didn't you read the welcome pack?'

'I flicked through it this morning but all I could see were instructions for the Rayburn cooker. There was nothing about the central heating boiler and I couldn't even find it. I lit the wood burner but I'm so cold, I think my fingers may drop off.'

He wasn't joking. Even in his coat pockets, his hands were like lumps of ice and, standing here on this dark, bitingly cold morning was doing him no favours.

'Well, come in then! Don't you have gloves?'

He blinked at her. 'I can't type with gloves on. I'm a writer. I like to pound out a couple of thousand words first thing in the morning. And thanks, but all I really want is for you to tell me where the thermostat is.'

'It's on the Rayburn.'

'The cooker?'

'It's not just a cooker. It heats the hot water and the radiators. Did you bank it up last night? Or refuel it?'

She was looking at him as if he should know what she

was talking about.

'I don't even know what that means. Bank it up? Refuel the cooker? With what?'

'It's not a cooker it's… Oh, for heaven's sake, come in. I'm freezing standing here. I'll make some coffee and explain. Then I'll get dressed and come in and sort you out.'

She walked away, clearly expecting him to follow.

'You're freezing!' he said. 'Imagine how I feel.'

She glanced back at him. 'Well, come in then. Unless you're frozen to the spot. You really should've read the welcome pack. It explains how everything works and it's there for a reason.'

So this was his fault? How did women do that? Make the man to blame for the problem. Bryony had been doing that for years.

Chapter Five

Holly led Gabriel into the kitchen and gave her sister a knowing look which she hoped Gabriel couldn't see.

'He didn't read the welcome pack and apparently, he's freezing to death.'

'Hello,' Ivy said, grinning. 'You must be the author.'

'And you must be the sister, based on the fact that you two look so much alike. Are you twins?'

Ivy nodded. 'Yes, but obviously not identical. Holly's the pretty one. I'm Ivy. Pleased to meet you.'

'I'm Gabriel and the pleasure's mine.'

Holly tutted, switching on the kettle. 'Don't talk rubbish, Ivy. You're the pretty one. Would you let him sit in the armchair so he can get warm?'

'You're both very pretty... and I'm fine—'

'You can sit on my lap if you like.' Ivy smiled and winked at Gabriel before jumping out of the battered but comfy armchair positioned to one side of the Rayburn.

'Oh. Um. Honestly, I'm fine now. It's like a furnace in here and I don't want to throw you out of your chair. You looked so comfortable, curled up with your coffee and a paper.'

'It's not a problem,' Ivy said. 'I need to go and take a shower soon, anyway. Please... sit down.'

Gabriel hesitated and Holly tutted once again.

'Sit down and get warm. How d'you take your coffee?'

Gabriel sat down. 'Thanks. I'll just get my hands warm. White with two sugars, please.'

Ivy scraped a wooden kitchen chair across the tiles,

31

plonked it in front of him and perched on the edge.

'Sugar's bad for you, you know,' she said.

'Lots of things are bad for me, but if I like them, I'm happy to take the risk.'

'Good for you. So I assume you didn't refuel the Rayburn before you went to bed.'

'No. But I didn't know I had to.'

'Should've read the welcome pack,' she teased.

'So I've been told. I'll do so the minute I go back.'

Ivy sipped her coffee and winked at Gabriel over the rim of her Christmassy mug.

'Actually, it's Holly's fault.'

'Thanks very much, Judas.' Holly banged two more Christmassy mugs on the worktop. Like Ivy's, these were covered with snowmen, robins and reindeers.

'What is?' Gabriel asked, his eyes darting from Holly to Ivy and back.

'She's supposed to make sure you read it. And she should've—'

'Thank you!' Holly snapped.

'Anytime.' Ivy beamed at her sister and gave Gabriel another wink.

Holly sighed. 'It is my fault, actually. I was expecting you to arrive much earlier so I lit the Rayburn first thing in the morning. I was going to refuel it when you arrived and give you a brief tutorial on how to use it. But you didn't arrive, and then I forgot about it and when you finally turned up, I was on my way to bed and… well, it slipped my mind. Sorry. I was going to pop in this morning and do it. But the radiators shouldn't be stone cold. There should've been enough heat left to keep them warm at the very least.'

She didn't like the way he was smiling at her.

'So it's not my fault then?'

She made the coffee and handed him his. 'Not entirely. But if you'd read the welcome pack, you could've done it yourself. Here. Have a mince pie. You left them here last night.' She tossed the tin across the table.

'Thanks, but no. The radiators were red hot when I went to bed. In fact if anything, the cottage was too warm, although it was wonderful to have a long, hot bath after getting soaked and half-frozen yesterday.'

'That explains it!' Holly said. 'You had a bath.'

'Is that a problem? Can't I have a bath and central heating too? Do I have to choose?'

'Of course not. You just have to refuel the Rayburn. I'll show you how and it won't happen again.'

'Mystery solved,' Ivy said. 'You killed the central heating with a bath. Don't you like mince pies? Holly's are fab. Although not quite as fab as Petunia's, apparently. You should try one.'

'Thanks but I'm saving myself for breakfast. Um. Do I need to refuel anything to cook that?'

'I'll cook you breakfast,' Holly said. 'If you want me to, that is. I'll cook breakfast, plus cakes for afternoon tea. For everything else, you fend for yourself.'

'I'm perfectly capable of throwing a couple of eggs in a pan. There's no need to trouble yourself.'

'I don't know,' Ivy said, grinning. 'You couldn't throw a couple of logs in the Rayburn... or read a welcome pack. I'd take Holly up on the offer if I were you. Here. Read this. It's the village newsletter. It'll tell you about all the madly exciting things you can see and do in Hideaway Down.' She passed him the newsletter and got to her feet. 'You won't know what to do first. Right. I'm off to take a shower... and then I'll refuel *this* Rayburn.'

'Thanks,' Gabriel said. 'I hope I haven't thrown you out of your cottage as well as your chair.'

33

'Huh? Oh you mean because it's called Ivy Cottage and I'm Ivy.'

Gabriel nodded. 'And this one's called Holly Cottage and Holly lives here.'

'Ivy doesn't live in Hideaway Down,' Holly said. 'She lives in London. We were named after the cottages though, I'm sad to say. Our mum's a tad… crazy.'

'It could've been worse,' Ivy said, looking at Gabriel. 'The other two cottages are called Mistletoe Cottage and Vine Cottage.'

Holly grinned. 'Mum's cat is called Mistletoe and her dog – a Red Setter – is called—'

'Don't tell me,' Gabriel interrupted, with a grin. 'The dog's called Vine.'

Holly shook her head. 'No. She's called Merlot.'

Gabriel frowned.

'The grape from the vine,' Ivy informed him. 'As Holly said, 'our mum's mad. Come into the pub later. The Snowdrop Inn. You can tell her all about Holly's lax attitude towards the paying guests. She'll love that. She might even buy you a drink. Although to be honest, she'd be more likely to tell you to get lost if you don't like the service. Very protective of her daughters is Janet Gilroy.'

Gabriel laughed. 'What about your dad? Will he throw me out on my ear too?'

Holly exchanged glances with Ivy. 'Dad's… no longer with us.'

'I'm so sorry. I didn't know.'

'He's not dead!' Ivy laughed.

'He is as far as Mum's concerned,' Holly said. 'So please don't mention him to her. Dad ran off to Spain five years ago after 'meeting' one of his ex-girlfriends on a social media site. Ivy and I go to see him, and he comes back to England to see us, but if he ever set foot in

Hideaway Down again, he'd find his heart on a stake in the middle of Market Field.'

'Not that you're interested in our family history,' Ivy added, giving Holly an odd look.

Holly blushed. 'Sorry. I don't know why I told you all that.'

'I'm glad you did,' Gabriel said, smiling. 'At least I won't upset your mum by saying the wrong thing.

Ivy gave a little cough. 'Right. I'm off for that shower. See you later. Missing you already.'

She disappeared into the hall and thudded up the stairs singing the words to *Baby, It's Cold Outside.*

'Mum's not the only Gilroy who's a little mad,' Holly said. 'Sorry about that.'

'No need to apologise. I think your sister's lovely.'

'Yeah. Most people do. Okay. I'll nip upstairs and throw on some clothes and then if you're warm enough now, we can go next door and I'll show you how to use the Rayburn. You can take the newsletter with you, if you like.'

'I'm overcome with excitement on both counts. Sorry. That was sarcastic, wasn't it?'

'A little, yes. But I have a feeling there's going to be a lot of that this Christmas, and I can give as good as I get.'

'I don't doubt that for a minute.' He smiled at her and stood up. 'I wasn't looking forward to this Christmas... but I think it may be better than I expected.'

What on earth did he mean by that? Holly threw him a look and headed towards the hall without another word.

Chapter Six

'You lost again?'

Gabriel spun on his heel and met the red faced farmer who'd helped him last night. From the beaming smile he was giving Gabriel, the man was a great deal happier to see him today than he had been last night.

Gabriel smiled back. 'Only in thought. I was admiring this wonderfully quaint Norman church. It wouldn't look out of place on a Christmas card. I hadn't realised how picturesque this village is. Mind you, I couldn't see much of it in the dark and the storm. Thanks again for helping me. I'd still be driving around those lanes if it hadn't been for you. I'm Gabriel, by the way. Gabriel Hardwick. Your name's Henry, I believe. Holly Gilroy told me.'

Henry took off his flat cap and fiddled with the peak – or bill, as Gabriel's dad called his. He had one almost identical to Henry's. Gabriel had bought it for him one Christmas, many years ago.

'Henry Goode and I'm happy to help. I expect the only thing you could see last night, was the hailstones and my muddy rear end. Well, the tractor's, anyway. You made it up the hill then?'

Gabriel nodded. 'Yep. And thankfully the storm died away just as I reached the cottages. I don't think I've been happier to see a cottage in my entire life. Which reminds me, I owe you a drink. Do you have plans for lunch? If not, I'd like to buy you a pie and a pint, or whatever you fancy at The Snowdrop Inn.'

Henry chuckled. 'I fancy the landlady. But don't tell the

wife that. She'll have me chopped up and stuffed in one of her brother's sausages before you can say minced pork. He's the village butcher.'

'My lips are sealed. Do you mean Janet Gilroy? I hadn't realised she was the landlady of a pub until her daughters told me. For some reason I'd assumed The Snowdrop Inn was... an inn, as in a bed and breakfast, although I have no idea why. I suppose it's because of the holiday cottages.'

Henry's heavy brows furrowed and he rubbed his stubble-covered chin. 'You're making about as much sense as Duck pudding. But I'll happily join you for lunch.'

'What's Duck pudding?'

'Precisely. Come with me, lad. I'll introduce you to some of the locals. And the lovely Janet Gilroy, of course. So where're you from then? And more to the point, why are you spending Christmas on your own in Hideaway Down?'

Gabriel fell into step beside him.

'I'm from Surrey. I'm an author and I've got a book to finish writing. I thought the solitude would help me do that.'

'No family? No pretty wife or girlfriend. Or will she be joining you later?'

Gabriel hesitated. 'I have a dad. That sounded daft. Everyone has a dad. What I meant was my mum died several years ago leaving just me, my sister, my dad and my gran. Until this year.' He swallowed down the lump in his throat. He still couldn't think of his gran without welling up. 'Gran died at the start of January and Dad, to my great surprise, got remarried in June. He's spending Christmas in the Alps with his new wife and her three kids.'

'Sorry about your mum and your gran. Time may be a great healer but we never stop missing them. Aren't you welcome in the Alps then? Or didn't you want to go?'

37

'I'm not great with kids and three is two too many to spend Christmas with. I was invited but I made my excuses. Dad understands and we'll meet up in the New Year. When I spoke to him yesterday, I got the feeling he was wishing he didn't have to be there either. He's sixty-five. The oldest stepdaughter is thirteen. Then there's another girl of eleven and the youngest, a boy, is nine.'

'Married a younger woman then?'

Gabriel smirked. 'Don't they always? She's forty. That's only five years older than me. I think he'll live to regret it but he was "smitten", to quote his word, and he only told me and my sister, Annabelle, a few days before the wedding. Annabelle likes Susie, the new wife but I'm reserving judgement. Like everyone, she has good points and not so good. All I care about is that she makes Dad happy and if she does that, then she's got my vote.'

'He's not happy yet then?'

'Not that I can tell.'

'And your sister? Where's she this Christmas?'

'Hawaii. With her husband's family. She's got two kids. A girl and a boy. And I do quite like them as it happens. But not enough to spend a whole two weeks with, day in, day out. Besides, I prefer my Christmases cold.'

'You and me both. And we're in luck. It's going to be a mighty cold one this year. The holly, mistletoe and other berry bushes are full to bursting, and that's a sure sign of a cold winter. Then there's the Gaggle Gang.'

'The what?'

'The geese.'

'The geese?' Gabriel had heard that a mass of berries predicted a harsh winter but geese were new to him.

Henry grinned. 'You'll meet them soon enough. Morning Bartram.' Henry waved one large hand at a portly man standing in the doorway of a shop across the street.

38

'That's my brother-in-law, Bartram, Beth's younger brother.'

Gabriel glanced over. The shop had a red-tiled frontage and a sign over the large single-paned window saying: Battersfold Butchers. Inside hung a variety of meat and fowl, along with strings of sausages, and in between, Christmas decorations on long, golden ribbons.

'He's very well-stocked,' Gabriel said.

'People travel from miles around to buy from Bartram. All the meat comes from local farms and it's all free range, organic or at the very least, outdoor reared. Most things you'll find in Hideaway Down are locally produced and to the highest standards. The General Store next door stocks all manner of goods and in the summer, there's a weekly market that's so popular we have to organise parking in one of my yards and bring the shoppers in by tractor-trailer. The tiny, village car park behind the shops can't cope. We do the same for the Christmas Market.'

'A Christmas Market? Really? I'd like to see that. When is it?'

'It's this Sunday. They're usually held in Market Field but that's under water so the Reverend's offered the church hall. Should be a good turnout.'

As they walked on, Gabriel took in the row of shops, tightly packed on either side of the street and crammed full of interesting and delightful items, many emitting tantalising smells that made his mouth water and his stomach rumble. The freshest produce he'd ever seen; scrumptious-looking cakes; heavenly scented soaps and candles. Even the hairdresser's looked inviting and the ironmonger's with the smithy on one side and a basket weaver's overflowing with traditional Sussex trugs on the other, were calling his name. He was certain of it. Hideaway Down was a hidden treasure for even the most demanding shopper. His sister, Annabelle would love it. He could do all his Christmas shopping in one place… if he hadn't already done it, or if he had anyone else to buy for.

Henry stopped suddenly. 'And here's The Snowdrop Inn.'

'Surely we didn't drive past this last night? How could I have missed it?'

'No. We came down Hideaway Lane from the north. That brings you into the village, halfway up Market Street which is this street. We crossed over and continued on down Hideaway Lane to the south, which took us to Hideaway Hill. Didn't you drive back down today then?'

Gabriel shook his head, still half mesmerised by the fifteenth-, possibly sixteenth-century, slightly askew façade of The Snowdrop Inn. 'I walked down via the footpath Holly told me about this morning. It brought me out at St Catherine's Church which was where you found me. This place is stunning.'

The Snowdrop Inn stood back from Market Street on a raised, lengthy bank of grass. There were a few wooden tables and chairs outside, unoccupied due to the freezing temperature, and what looked to Gabriel like a chestnut tree, bare now of course but he could picture it in spring alive with pink and white blossoms and in autumn, hanging heavy with conkers.

To one side of the long, two-storey pub, the bank sloped down to a pond; not large but big enough for several people to skate on if it ever froze over. At the moment there were small islands of ice but even from this distance, Gabriel could tell they were tiny slivers. Beyond the pond lay a large field, most of which was under two or three inches of water. It was fenced off from a narrow pavement and had 'Market Field' in large iron letters on an intricately designed iron gate; no doubt the work of the local

40

blacksmith.

'This village should win 'The prettiest village in England' award,' Gabriel said, following Henry to the pub. 'It's like stepping back into a bygone era.'

'And have even more people invade it in the summer? No thanks,' Henry replied, opening the black plank door to the sound of the tinkling bells on the overhead beam.

A cacophony of voices, mixed with carols ringing out from speakers on the walls, almost deafened Gabriel after the peace and tranquillity of the village outside. This was the heart of Hideaway Down, there was no doubt of that. Two large, log fires burned brightly at either end of the pub and mouth-watering smells wafted in from somewhere behind the bar, at which a row of people perched on high, wooden stools, chatted happily. Above them were row upon row of twinkling, multi-coloured lights and decorations of every shape and size cavorted in the breeze which accompanied Gabriel and Henry's entrance.

'Is it always this busy?' Gabriel asked, looking round at several wooden tables all fully occupied.

'This is quiet for a Saturday,' Henry said. 'Must be the cold weather keeping folks indoors. Let's find a table. Then I'll introduce you to the lovely Janet Gilroy.'

Chapter Seven

'Hey, Gabriel!'

'Don't call him over.' Holly glowered at her sister. 'I'm trying to have a quiet drink, happy in the knowledge that, if your news last night based on village gossip, is correct – and the gossip always is – Paul won't be back in Hideaway Down until Sunday evening.'

Ivy play-punched her in the arm. 'Of course it's right. But as for a quiet drink... In here? You are kidding? Anyway, you can still do that. I'll talk to Gabriel. You don't have to. I see he's with Henry. He's made a friend already.'

Gabriel smiled and he and Henry wandered over.

'Hello Ivy. And Holly, too. This is a nice surprise.'

'It's the only pub in the village,' Holly said. 'So not so surprising when you think about it.'

'You in one of your moods, Hollyberry?' Henry pulled her to him in a bear hug.

She threw him what she hoped was a quelling look when he released her but as he burst out laughing, it couldn't have been as 'quelling' as she'd intended.

'Did the other guests arrive?' Gabriel asked, giving her a rather odd look of his own. 'How many are there?'

'In Mistletoe Cottage there's a family with young kids and in Vine, a couple with a dog. They all seem very nice, so I'm not sure why you're pulling a face.'

'Was I?' Gabriel's eyes darted from Holly to Henry then Ivy and back to Holly.

Ivy nodded. 'Yeah. You looked a bit like this.' She

opened her eyes wide, stuck out her tongue as if she were about to be sick and screwed up her nose and mouth.

Gabriel laughed. 'I did not! You look as if your face has been squashed against a brick wall.'

'He's not too fond of children,' Henry said. 'Oh. That wasn't a secret, was it?'

'No. No secret. And I'm not a lover of dogs either.'

'Well, you're in for a treat then,' Ivy said.

'Or mince pies,' Holly muttered. 'At least the new guests read the welcome pack.'

'Who's not a lover of dogs?'

As if on cue, a large Red Setter came bounding out from behind the door Janet Gilroy had swung open. The dog's furry ears flapped like stunted wings as she took off through the crowded bar, nearly knocking Gabriel over. Merlot was swiftly followed by Mistletoe, the tortoiseshell cat.

'One of our guests, Mum,' Holly said, laughing. 'This is Gabriel Hardwick. Gabriel, this is our mum, Janet and those two are Merlot and Mistletoe.'

'The author who got lost last night?' Janet enquired, with a smile.

'That's the one,' Henry said.

'Well, at least you've managed to find your way to our pub. That's the important thing. I'm pleased to meet you, Gabriel. Have you settled in? Please let me know if you've got any problems. Actually, let Holly know. She's running the cottages.'

Gabriel seemed a little shell-shocked. Mistletoe had taken a shortcut in her pursuit of Merlot and jumped on the bar, hissed at Gabriel whose elbow was in her way and careered over his shoulder, rather than go round.

'What just happened?' he said, blinking several times.

'Sorry. Um. It's good to meet you, Janet.'

43

Janet beamed at him. 'Oh don't worry about Mistletoe. She'll be rubbing her head against you and curling up on your lap in no time. She likes to chase the dog and Merlot's happy to oblige.'

From the look in Gabriel's dark eyes, Holly got the feeling he didn't relish the prospect of either.

'Good to know. And no, I don't have any problems, thanks. Holly very kindly showed me how the Rayburn worked. I thought it was merely a cooker. I had no idea it also housed a boiler for the hot water and the central heating, although the pack makes that clear, once you've read it. The cottage is perfect and I managed to get a few hours' writing done this morning. It's so peaceful up there.'

'Not for long,' Ivy quipped. 'Two kids and a dog may change all that.' She glanced down the length of the bar. 'Why is Ned Stelling waving at me?'

'Perhaps he'd like a drink after working over the blistering heat of a forge all morning,' Holly suggested. 'This is a pub after all and you're a barmaid.'

Ivy grinned. 'I thought there was something else I should be doing. Catch you later. Okay, okay. Hold your horseshoes, Ned. I'm coming.'

'I'd best get on, too,' Janet said. 'I hope we'll see you in here at least once a day, Gabriel. Are you staying for lunch? I'll organise a table if you are.'

'Thanks. That'd be great. Would you like to join us, Holly?'

'Me? Er. No thanks. I mean… I've got lots to do. Er. Shopping and stuff.'

'Maybe see you later?'

Why was he looking at her like that? When she'd shown him how to use the Rayburn he'd looked at her in the same way. A bit like Merlot had when the dog had arrived from the rescue centre; wary but curious; eager to be friends yet

44

also wanting to keep a distance. There was something in Gabriel's eyes, almost as if, like Merlot, he was hoping for a second chance in life.

She must be imagining it. Perhaps it was just the way he looked at everyone.

'Maybe. I have to go now. Um. I've just remembered something I'd forgotten. Enjoy your lunch. Bye Henry. Give my love to Beth.'

'Will do. Does that mean we won't be seeing you in here tonight then?' Henry frowned at her. 'He's not worth it, Hollyberry. You can do better. Much better. Besides, I heard he's not arriving until tomorrow. And Janet said she'd chuck the both of them in the pond if they set foot over the threshold.'

'Thanks, Henry. I know.'

Her cheeks were on fire and from the expression on Gabriel's face, he was about to start asking questions. She flung on her coat, buried her head in the collar and dashed for the door.

Wonderful. It was bad enough that the entire village knew about her disastrous love life. Now Gabriel Hardwick would know about it too. Henry would make sure of that. And if he didn't, someone else probably would. Then Gabriel would think she was even more of a pathetic loser than he possibly already did.

For some peculiar reason, that mattered.

Chapter Eight

Holly ambled around the village popping into each and every shop. She didn't need anything; she just wanted to browse around and this would be the last chance she'd get. She'd be at the Christmas Market or helping her mum, tomorrow and after that… Well, as Paul and Naomi were due to arrive tomorrow night, she'd be spending as much time as possible hiding away in her cottage.

Why didn't that prospect seem as bad today as it had only yesterday? Nothing had changed. She was still in love with Paul, the man who'd dumped her the moment he'd met her best friend.

Okay. It wasn't *the moment* he'd met Naomi. They had known each other for about two years. But what was two years when he and Holly had known each other all their lives and been dating since they were fifteen?

Would she ever be able to forgive them for their betrayal? She often felt that it would have been better if they'd just come out and told her instead of sneaking around behind her back and then running off on New Year's Eve without so much as a word. Unless you counted the long note they had left. And even that mocked her because instead of each of them explaining individually why they treated her with such contempt, they're written the note together and signed it: *Lots of love from Naomi and Paul, and we're really, really sorry.*

Yeah, right.

'You don't seem to have bought anything.'

Gabriel's voice made Holly jump.

'Oh. I... I can't decide what I want. Did you enjoy your lunch?'

'Yes thanks. And your mum was right. Mistletoe did come and try to curl up on my lap.'

Holly met his eyes and grinned. 'Tried?'

Gabriel shrugged his broad shoulders. 'Let's just say that I explained to her how difficult it was for me to eat with a bundle of fur turning circles on my lap. She finally agreed and settled on my coat.'

Holly examined the navy cashmere. Together with the trace of a white line left by Holly's toothpaste, which was still visible from this close, Mistletoe's red, brown and cream hairs were dotted all over the front.

'Oh dear.' She fought back her laughter. It really wasn't funny. That coat was clearly expensive.

'It's not my favourite coat,' he said, as if reading her mind. 'In fact I'm not attached to it at all, having only bought it last week. May I walk with you?' He grinned.

'That sounded very formal. Rather like in the old days when men asked to walk out with their beaus.'

Holly studied his face. 'How much did you have to drink?'

'Um... two pints. Why?'

'No reason. Don't you want to get back to your writing?'

He pulled a face as if to say he couldn't care less.

'It can wait. It's such a gorgeous day after yesterday, isn't it?'

He tipped his head back and closed his eyes and Holly stood looking up at him. The afternoon sun picked several locks of deep, dark brown hair to illuminate whilst the bitingly cold breeze lifted a few strands from his forehead, and brought a healthy glow to his cheeks. Holly's eyes traced the outline of his firm, clean-shaven jaw before

47

taking in the sensual curve of his lips. Hers parted in a mirror-reflection of his and her heart rattled against the bars of its cage.

Suddenly, his dark lashes flickered and he opened his eyes, staring directly into Holly's.

'Gorgeous,' she repeated, finding it hard to catch her breath after far too many seconds of them staring at one another.

'Absolutely,' he replied.

'Don't take up the whole pavement, sweetheart.'

'Oh! Sorry, Gramps. I was... I didn't see you coming.'

'Don't suppose you did.' Gramps grinned and looked Gabriel up and down. 'You must be the author who got lost last night. I'm Gordon Gilroy, Holly's grandad. But everyone calls me Gramps. I'm the oldest man in Hideaway Down, you know. Bet that surprised you. You're probably thinking I don't look a day over sixty but I'm eighty-four. I can tell you some tales if you're stuck for ideas for your books. Some of them are quite juicy. Make that Fifty Shades of Green seem tame, some of them would. So what do you think of our little village? And what about our Holly? She's a stunner, isn't she?'

'Gramps! And it's Fifty Shades of Grey not... oh never mind.'

Holly's cheeks burned as she shot Gabriel a look but he was smiling warmly at her grandfather.

'I am surprised by your age and I may take you up on your offer, thanks. I think the village is possibly the prettiest I've ever seen and—'

'So where're you off to?' Holly interrupted.

She'd rather not know what he thought of her. Especially as he'd made it pretty clear how much he liked Ivy. The pair of them had seemed to hit it off the moment they met.

Gramps frowned. 'You're a bright girl, sweetheart. I'm sure you can figure it out by what I'm wearing.'

Holly tutted. 'Well obviously you're going fishing. What I really meant was, isn't it a bit late in the day to be heading out to Hideaway Hole? Besides it's absolutely freezing and getting colder by the second. You'll probably freeze to death and end up looking like one of those fishing gnomes Sarah Saltcote loves so much. She'll have you moved into her garden.'

Gramps' green eyes twinkled. 'There's worse fates than ending up in Sarah Saltcote's garden, sweetheart. As a matter of fact, I quite like the notion. Must be off. And don't you worry about me. I've got my trusty friend and I won't be more than an hour or so. Be home before the sun sets.'

He tapped his breast pocket, where Holly knew he kept his flask of whisky, tipped his large tweed hat at Gabriel and trotted up Market Street whistling a happy tune, as if he were no older than a teenager.

'He's right,' Gabriel said. 'He doesn't look his age and what a friendly man.'

'He doesn't act it either. He's mad to go fishing in this weather but there's no point in trying to stop him. He'll do exactly what he wants when he wants, regardless of anyone else's opinion.'

'What and where is Hideaway Hole?'

'It's a small, natural lake that's fed by one of the rivers hereabouts. No one's absolutely sure which one as it's nestled between four hills, one of which is Hideaway Hill which leads, as you know, up to Hideaway Cliff. We think there's an underwater tributary. There's a tiny waterfall of sorts which trickles down a section of Hideaway Cliff into the sea. It's called The Old Woman's Tap. In the summer it just drips but in the winter it flows, like a tap.'

'I'd like to see that. Both the lake and the waterfall.'

'Don't get too excited. They're just a small lake and a plume of water running from the cliff face, not exactly Niagara Falls and the Great Lakes. But if you're really interested, ask Gramps. He'd love to show you. Right. I must get back. I've got cakes to bake for afternoon tea. You clearly don't like mince pies, so tell me what you do like and I'll see if I can make it.'

Gabriel looked surprised. 'There's no need to go to any trouble on my account. I don't need afternoon tea.'

'It's no trouble and I'm doing it for the other guests anyway so…' She shrugged. 'It's there if you want it. Do you like cupcakes?'

'I like anything.'

'But not mince pies.'

Holly stepped off the pavement and Gabriel fell into step beside her.

'I do like mince pies.' His voice was low and it crackled with emotion. 'It's just… they were my gran's favourite and we always made them together at this time of year. It was a tradition throughout my life and… it feels odd to eat someone else's. That sounds weird, I suppose.'

Holly stopped and looked at him. 'No, it doesn't. I assume your gran's no longer with you. Was it recent?'

He nodded. 'Fairly. She passed away in January. But it feels like only yesterday sometimes. Especially at the moment.'

'I'm sorry for your loss. Were you very close?'

'Extremely. I was even named after her. She was the reason I became an author. She… encouraged me. But she had a wonderfully full life and no regrets. How many of us can say that?'

'Not many and certainly not me. Um. I've got my car in the car park. It's just through this twitten.' She pointed to the narrow cobbled alley between Battersfold Butchers and The General Store. If you're heading back to Ivy Cottage I'll give you a lift up the hill.'

'Thanks. I wasn't really looking forward to the walk back up. I don't think I'm as fit as I thought I was. Too much sitting on my backside hunched over a laptop.'

Holly led the way through to her rather ancient Mini.

'What do you write? I don't recall seeing any 'Gabriel Hardwick' books. Or do you use a pen name?'

'You could say that. I mean. I'm a ghostwriter. That means—'

'You write about the paranormal.' Holly grinned at him over the roof of her car. 'I'm joking. I know what a ghostwriter is. You write for other people. I managed a book shop in Eastbourne for almost ten years.'

'Managed? You don't any longer? You used the past tense.'

They got in and Holly rested her forearms on the wheel. 'I was made redundant at the end of November. It was an independent book store and the owner felt it was no longer viable. He decided it was time to retire and he closed the shop. He said he'd been thinking about it for almost a year but he hadn't wanted to tell me because he knew how... um... Never mind that. Anyway, these things happen and he gave me quite a good redundancy package.'

'That must've been rough. So you're helping your mum whilst you decide on your future career path? Any ideas what that might be?'

She sighed and started the car. 'None whatsoever. But there's a big, bright world full of opportunities out there. At least that's what Ivy tells me. I'm just hoping she's right.'

Chapter Nine

Gabriel nipped upstairs to change out of his sweater and into a T-shirt. He had been writing in the kitchen since returning from the village with Holly, and was feeling decidedly warm. Now that he had learnt how to use the Rayburn, the cottage was hotter than Hawaii; and his sister had told him earlier, it was twenty-five degrees Celsius there.

Passing in front of the window, he glanced out and the view took his breath away. Against an ice blue sky, it looked as if the sun was setting into a bed of multi-coloured blankets, piled one on top of another in shades of pink, pale orange, red, purple and deep violet. It cast a silver glow across a stretch of sea the colour of melted mercury.

Last night he'd been too tired to look outside and had merely drawn the curtains, not that he would have seen much in the pitch black. This morning, he had other things on his mind, like the heating and going next door to see Holly. He had thrown on his clothes and pulled back the curtains without a second thought. If he'd realised the view was this spectacular, he would have gone outside and watched the sunrise, albeit in the freezing cold.

He heard the doorbell and with a final glance at the sunset, turned away and dashed downstairs.

'Christmas cupcakes,' Holly said, holding up a plate of little cakes made to look like snowmen and women. 'It's white butter icing on a chocolate sponge cake, with marshmallows for the heads. The eyes, hats and scarves are shaped from sweets and melted chocolate. Every bit of it is edible except for the Christmassy paper case.'

'They're incredible, Holly. Thank you. You shouldn't have gone to so much trouble though.'

'It was no trouble. I was making them anyway, for the children next door.'

'I see. Well, thanks. They look delicious. Would you like to come in?'

'No thanks. Ivy's back from the pub and insisting that we put some decorations up before her shift this evening. Oh! What happened to your hand? Are you okay?'

Gabriel had forgotten his wound as he reached out his hand. He quickly took the plate of cakes and smiled.

'It's nothing. I'm fine.'

'It doesn't look like "nothing". How did you do it?'

'I burnt it on the Rayburn.'

'The cooker?'

'It's not just a cooker,' he said, with a grin. 'It's an instrument of torture. I forgot the hotplate would be… hot.'

'Perhaps I'd better cook breakfast for you every day during your stay, and any other meals you plan to eat here. Or you could eat in the village. Either that or you could hang a note on the Rayburn saying: 'Hot. Proceed with caution'.' Holly laughed and shook her head.

Gabriel smiled and watched Holly's green eyes twinkle; her cheeks flushed like rose-coloured Christmas baubles; her cherry-brandy lips parted over perfect teeth; her hair, the colour of roasted chestnuts danced around her shoulders. It wasn't just the Rayburn that should have a sign saying: 'Hot. Proceed with caution'.

'I'm sorry,' she said. 'I shouldn't make fun of you. You'll be fine once you get used to it.'

'That's the first time I've heard you laugh. It sounds like little silver bells. You should do it more often. It's lovely. And as for you cooking for me, I think I could get used to

53

that. How about dinner tonight?'

She blinked several times and her rose-coloured cheeks turned vivid red. He had embarrassed her. He'd said too much.

'Er... I'm making a casserole for me and Ivy. You're welcome to come and join us for that.'

He should say no. He should give her some space. Especially after what Henry had told him in the pub today about her ex-boyfriend, Paul and the fact that she was still in love with him. Besides, he had only recently got out of a rather intense relationship himself and one that still had several complications. He needed to tread carefully. The last thing he was looking for was another romantic entanglement.

'I'd love to. What time? And didn't you say that you and Ivy will be putting up decorations? I can help with that.'

What was wrong with him? Why hadn't he just said no? And now she was avoiding his eyes. She seemed to be looking everywhere except at him.

'There's no need. Unless you want to, of course.'

'I want to,' he said.

Her eyelids flickered upwards. 'We're starting as soon as I get back. You can come whenever you want.'

'I'll be there in ten minutes. I'll bring a bottle of wine. Do you prefer red or white? I've got both.'

Why was he finding it difficult to breathe? This wasn't a date or anything. Just two people putting up decorations and eating supper. Three people. Ivy would be there.

'I like both. I'll leave it up to you. I'd better get back.'

The tiniest smile crept across her mouth and he was sure that, if she hadn't turned and strode down the path at that very second, he would have grabbed her by the shoulders and kissed her for all he was worth.

He must be coming down with something. This wasn't

like him at all. You only found passion like that in the pages of romance novels.

Chapter Ten

'What's up with you?' Ivy asked, as Holly rushed into the kitchen and headed towards the sink. 'Your cheeks are as red as a Santa suit.'

'It's freezing out there.'

'And that's why you're splashing cold water on your face, is it?'

'Oh. Um. It's warm water,' Holly lied.

'Yes. And I'm one of Santa's elves. Does this have something to do with gorgeous Gabriel?'

'No!'

'That's a yes then. You should've asked him to help us put up the Christmas decorations and stay for dinner after.'

Holly dabbed her face dry with a Christmas-tree patterned towel and cleared her throat.

'I did. He's coming round in ten minutes and he's bringing wine.'

'That's more like it.' Ivy beamed at Holly. 'Would you like me to make myself scarce? I'm sure I can find someone to go and annoy.'

'No! I need you here.'

'*Need* me here? Why? What are you frightened of? I don't think Gabriel will bite. Well, not in a bad way, if you know what I mean. I thought I noticed a little spark between the two of you.'

'What? It's not me he likes, it's you.'

Ivy frowned. 'Sometimes Holly, you say the most ridiculous things. I wouldn't mind betting that by the end of this evening, if you play your cards right, you won't be wrapping mini Christmas cakes to hand out at The Snowdrop Bash on Christmas Eve, you'll be wrapping your arms around Gabriel's heavenly body.'

Holly's jaw dropped, like the branch of a Christmas tree bearing a heavy bauble.

'I'll be doing no such thing. And you seem to be forgetting, I'm still in love with Paul.'

'How could I possibly forget that? Sorry. That was bitchy. I didn't mean that. But you do have to face facts, Holly. As awful as it may be, Paul is with Naomi now, and he's bringing her home to do the 'Family Christmas' thing. That means it's pretty serious.'

'No, it doesn't. We spent Christmas together every year for fifteen years.'

'Yes. But he had Christmas dinner at his house and you had Christmas dinner at Mum's. You just spent Christmas afternoon and evening together.'

'Are you *trying* to hurt me?'

'I'm *trying* to make you see sense. What's the point in pining over someone you can't have, when there's a red-blooded, hot-bodied hunk of a man in the cottage next door, who there's a very good chance, you can have? And unless I'm mistaken, that's him ringing the doorbell now. He can't even wait for ten minutes to see you again. I'll let him in, shall I?'

Holly grabbed the bottle of wine Ivy had opened last night and poured herself a large glass, taking three rapid gulps. She put it on the kitchen table and used her fingers as a makeshift comb to tidy her hair before pulling out a chair. She sat up straight and took several deep breaths. She could hear Ivy and Gabriel laughing in the hall and she knew she had been right. It was Ivy Gabriel liked, not her. Not that it mattered. As she had told Ivy, she was still in love with Paul.

57

'Hello again.' Gabriel smiled at her as he entered the kitchen. 'I had one of your cupcakes. It was delicious. If the rest of your baking is that good, you should start a cake-making enterprise.'

'Thanks. There's already a bakery in the village. It's owned by Maisy Miller. Besides, I'm more of a home cook. There's nothing particularly special about my baking. Or anything else for that matter.'

'I can't agree with that. And I bumped into Robin, the dad in Mistletoe Cottage, just now. The first thing he mentioned was how good your cupcakes were.'

'Tea, Gabriel?' Ivy asked, switching on the kettle. 'There's coffee or hot chocolate if you prefer. Or wine. It may only be around four o'clock but I see Holly has started.'

'Somewhere in the world, it's evening,' Holly said.

'Tea please,' Gabriel said. 'Just in case I have to climb any ladders to hang the decorations. I brought both red and white for later. You can take your pick.'

He put a bag on the table and Ivy peered in.

'Are you trying to get us drunk? Two bottles of each.'

Gabriel laughed. 'No. What we don't drink today, you can drink another time. What's the plan with the decorations? Inside and out? Or don't you do the twinkling lights thing?'

'You can usually see this cottage from the space station at Christmas,' Ivy said. 'Things have been a bit... hectic this year and Holly hasn't had any time to do them.'

'Well, it won't take long with three of us.'

Holly jumped to her feet. 'And the sooner we get started, the sooner we'll be finished. I'll get the boxes from the loft.'

Gabriel reached out and his hand brushed her arm.

'I'll get the boxes from the loft. Just show me the way.'

Holly shrugged. 'Okay, thanks. Follow me.'

'To the ends of the earth... Er. As the saying goes.'

'I'll have the coffee ready when you get back,' Ivy said, before breaking into a rendition of *It's Beginning to Look a Lot Like Christmas.*

'I don't suppose you really felt in a festive mood after being made redundant,' Gabriel said, following Holly up the stairs.

'No, I didn't. But it wasn't just the redundancy. Did Henry say anything about me over lunch?'

'A little. He mentioned that you'd had a long-term relationship, that it ended last New Year's Eve and that your best friend was involved in the break-up. He also said your ex was coming back for Christmas. Do you... still have feelings for him?'

'Yes. But Ivy's pretty much told me I don't stand a snowball's chance of getting him back.'

'Would you want him back?' Gabriel sounded surprised.

'Yes. Fifteen years is a long time to throw away.'

'Even after what he's done? And he didn't seem to think so.'

Holly spun round to face him at the top of the stairs.

'Henry clearly did a lot more than *mention* it, didn't he?'

Gabriel nodded. 'He told me quite a bit. I suppose I shouldn't have listened. Sorry.'

Holly waved her arm in the air.

'Why shouldn't you know? Everyone else does. Did he tell you how they met? Paul and Naomi?'

She tugged a cord, attached to the wall by a hook, and the loft hatch swung open.

'No. He didn't tell me that.'

Gabriel took the pole Holly passed him and pulled down the loft ladder.

'Naomi and I met at a yoga class in Eastbourne, hit it off

straight away and became best friends. Or so I thought. A few weeks later, she asked me if Paul and I would go with her and a guy from where she worked, on a double date, in case the guy turned out to be a jerk. Well, it seems I was the jerk. The minute she and Paul met everything changed, although I didn't realise it at the time. The rest, as they say, is history, as was her date. Paul and she started seeing one another behind my back and last New Year's Eve, just before the stroke of midnight funnily enough, they decided to spend their future together, and ran off. I haven't seen, or heard from them since. Although they did leave me a note.'

'A note! He didn't even have the decency to tell you to your face? And you want this guy back? You must really love him.'

'I do. The decorations are up there. The boxes are marked: 'Xmas Decs'. Don't bang your head on the roof timbers.'

Gabriel was looking at her as if she'd stolen Christmas.

'I'm sorry, Holly. I had no right to say that. It's none of my business.'

'No, it isn't. But that doesn't stop everyone else from having an opinion, so why not you? Shall I go up and get the boxes?'

'No. I'll get them.'

Gabriel climbed the ladder, and one by one, passed the boxes down to Holly. Ivy came up and helped carry the boxes downstairs to the sitting room before making Gabriel the coffee she had promised him.

'We'll need a tree,' Ivy said. 'I'll get one tomorrow at the Christmas Market. You can get one for your cottage if you like, Gabriel.'

He smiled. 'If you and Holly promise to come and help decorate it, I will.'

'It's a deal,' Ivy said. 'Did you tell the other guests

about the Christmas Market, Holly? They might want to put decorations up in their cottages too.'

'No. But I gave them a village newsletter. I'll mention it in the morning.'

Ivy smiled at Gabriel. 'We never decorate the cottages, other than a wreath on the door, in case the guests are Christmas-haters. Some people are, you know. Can't understand it myself. Any excuse to make merry is my motto.'

Gabriel nodded. 'I love Christmas. Although this is the first one without my grandmother. As I told Holly earlier, my gran passed away in January. But let's not dwell on that. Where shall I start?'

'I'm sorry,' Ivy said. 'Let's put on some Christmas music to get us in the festive spirit. I think we should start outside before it gets too dark to see.'

Holly switched on the TV and set it to one of the music channels playing Christmas music videos.

'If we're putting up the lights, we can switch them on and hang them. That way we'll be able to see what we're doing.'

Ivy grinned at her. 'Good thinking.'

As they made their way outside, a Collie came bounding up the path towards them.

'Hello, Bonnie!' Holly bent down and petted the excited dog. 'Where're your mum and dad?'

'Is she from Vine?' Ivy asked, nodding her head towards that cottage.

'Yes. She must have got out somehow. I'll just pop her back.'

Holly slipped her fingers through Bonnie's collar and led her to the door of Vine Cottage.

'Oh my goodness!' Beryl Davis was evidently surprised to find her dog outside. 'I'm so sorry. She must have nipped past me when I opened the back door.'

'It's not a problem,' Holly assured her. 'But the cliff edge isn't that far and there's a sharp drop in places. I'd hate for her to go over the edge. It's never happened before but there's always a first time.'

'Yes, of course. I should've been more careful. She's a good dog and very obedient but it only takes a minute for an accident to happen. We'll keep an eye on her. Thank you.'

'What's happened?' Beryl's husband, Bill came and placed a hand on his wife's shoulder.

'Nothing, thank goodness but Bonnie was outside. Holly kindly brought her back.'

'Good heavens. Sorry about that, love.'

'Please don't worry. It's really not a problem. My mum's got a dog so I know how easily they can slip out. I hope you're settling in okay.'

'It's perfect,' Beryl said, glancing at her husband with love in her eyes.

Holly smiled. 'There's a Christmas Market tomorrow. It's usually held outside in Market Field but due to the bad weather it'll probably be in the church hall. People come from miles around and the stalls sell everything from handmade Christmas decorations to organic cheese. There're food stalls, hot drinks, including mulled wine; stalls selling toys and gifts, many made by local craftsmen. There'll be holly, mistletoe and Christmas trees for sale. It's well worth a look. It starts at ten and ends around nine and most people end up in The Snowdrop Inn afterwards.'

'We'll definitely go to that, won't we, love?'

Beryl nodded. 'We'll be there. And Bonnie will be on her lead. And her best behaviour. I see you're putting up decorations.'

'Yes. They're usually up long before now but... we're

running late this year. You're welcome to put up decorations. We leave it up to people in each cottage to decide.'

'That'd be nice, Bill. We could pick something up at the market tomorrow.'

Bill nodded then smiled at Holly. 'D'you need a hand, love? Nothing like putting up decorations to get you in the festive mood.'

'I think we're okay, thanks.'

Did their smiles just drop? Holly glanced across at Ivy and Gabriel. Ivy had wrapped a string of coloured lights around herself. She waved at Holly and belted out the first words of the song *Oh Christmas Tree.*

'But you're welcome to come and help if you like,' Holly added.

'We'd love to,' Beryl said.

'Bring Bonnie. I think I heard Gabriel say that he liked dogs. He's staying in Ivy Cottage, and that's my sister, Ivy.'

Holly had no idea why she had lied about Gabriel liking dogs but it was too late now; Beryl, Bill and Bonnie Davis were keen to have some Christmas cheer.

Chapter Eleven

'You told them I like dogs,' Gabriel said, passing the final stack of dirty dishes to Holly.

'Did I?' Feigning ignorance was probably her best bet.

'Yes. Bill told me. Was that to pay me back for poking my nose into your business?'

Holly shrugged. 'I don't know why I said it. It just came out. You did seem to like her though.'

Holly didn't know what she had expected Gabriel to do, but playing tug-of-war with Bonnie before stroking her belly wasn't top of her list. Nor was him offering to make mulled wine for all of them... except Bonnie.

Gabriel smiled. 'It's the ones that won't stop barking I don't like. Bonnie hardly barked at all and when she did, it was a pleasant bark.'

'A pleasant bark? Surely a bark's a bark?' Holly giggled.

'Nah-uh. This is a pleasant bark.' He made a soft woof. 'This is an unpleasant bark.' He made three loud, high-pitched woofs.

'Yes, I see.' Holly tried not to laugh.

'What on earth is going on in here?' Ivy gave them both a quizzical look.

'Gabriel was singing. I didn't have the heart to tell him he sounded like a dog.'

Gabriel's eyes narrowed momentarily but the smile tugging at his mouth betrayed him.

Ivy grinned. 'Beryl and Bill are lovely, aren't they? And Bonnie's a delight. Even you seem to like her, Gabriel.'

'She's got a pleasant bark, apparently,' Holly said.

'I'm not even going to ask you to explain that.' Ivy pulled on her coat. 'Right I've got to love you and leave you. I'm needed in the pub. I told Mum I'd be in late tonight but she's texted me to say it's really busy, and as we finished putting up the decorations much earlier than expected, I told her I'd be there.'

'I think I might come with you.' Holly closed the door of the dishwasher and pushed the start button. 'It's only seven-thirty and it's a beautiful night. I'll come down with you in the car and walk back.'

'Are you mad? It was freezing when we were outside and that was more than two hours ago. You wouldn't get me going out on a night like this unless I had to. Which I do.'

'Would you mind if I went with you?' Gabriel asked.

'Don't you have a book to write?'

'Yes, Holly, I do. But as you said, it's a beautiful night, and a bracing walk up a very steep hill, I'm sure will do me the world of good.'

'Let's go then,' Ivy said.

Holly hesitated. She'd suggested going with Ivy so that she wouldn't be alone with Gabriel, not because she wanted to go to the pub on a freezing cold night. She could say she'd changed her mind. But in a way, tonight would be her last night of freedom, so perhaps she should go. Paul would be back in Hideaway Down tomorrow.

'I'll get my coat,' Holly said, heading towards the hall.

Gabriel followed behind. Holly passed his coat to him and all three marched outside, a bitingly cold wind hitting them full in the face.

'That's coming from the North,' Holly said. She pulled her coat tighter and shoved her gloved hands in her pockets.

'I forgot something.' Ivy stopped in her tracks. 'You go

65

on without me. I'll see you at the car.' She turned back towards the cottage.

'Bloody hell, it's cold.' Gabriel flipped his collar up before he too, pushed his hands inside his pockets.

'Don't you have gloves?' Holly asked.

'I think I left them at home. In Surrey I mean. I should've bought some today but it was such glorious weather that I forgot how cold it was. Perhaps I'll get some tomorrow at the Christmas Market.'

They walked down the path and round to the side of Holly Cottage to the gravel-covered parking area for Holly and Ivy cottages. There was an identical area at the side of Vine Cottage for Mistletoe and Vine cottages.

'Nice car,' Holly said. 'Love the colour.'

She hadn't paid much attention to it earlier. She'd been busy cleaning, baking and welcoming the new guests for most of the morning. When she dashed to her car to head down to the village, she only gave Gabriel's a cursory glance. She wasn't really sure what a dark red, convertible sports car said about a man.

A waxing moon, now three quarters full, shone a spotlight on the bonnet and below that, onto the grille, displaying the distinctive Jaguar badge. *That* said a great deal about the man – or at least about his money.

'Thanks. It's called *Caldera Red.* The car was actually my gran's. She hadn't had it long but she's always loved Jaguars.'

Holly hadn't expected that.

'Your gran's?'

Gabriel nodded. 'Yes. She left it to me in her will.'

'Wow. My gran left me a brooch. That badge alone probably cost more. Not that it's about the money. Although it would be nice to have some.'

'I can't argue with that. Gran came from working-class

66

stock though, and every penny she owned, she made herself. Grandad was an artist, and unfortunately not a particularly well-known one. Gran was the breadwinner in that marriage.'

'Okay, let's go.' Ivy dashed towards them. 'I don't know what you're standing out here for. The car is open.'

They all got in and Ivy did a three-point turn, revving the accelerator, slamming on the brakes and narrowly missing Gabriel's driver's door.

'Be careful, Ivy!' Holly shrieked. 'That car's worth around £100,000.'

'Cool. Any chance I could drive it, Gabriel?'

'If this is a demonstration of your driving, that would be a no.'

Ivy grinned at him in the rear view mirror. 'No sense of adventure?'

'That would also be a no.'

With a screech of tyres, Ivy tore down Hideaway Hill and in less than three minutes, she swerved into the car park at the rear of The Snowdrop Inn.

'It'll take you much longer to get back up that hill,' she said, as they got out of the car.

'I think part of me is still at the top of that hill,' Gabriel replied.

'I like you, Gabriel Hardwick. I thought you might be a pompous prat but you're not. You seem like a really decent guy.'

'Ivy!' Holly cringed with embarrassment.

Gabriel raised his brows. 'Thanks. I think.' He smiled. 'I like you too. I like both of you. A lot.'

'Everyone does,' Ivy said, shoving the pub door open with her bottom as she turned back and beamed at Gabriel and Holly.

Once inside, Ivy left them.

'Is she always happy?' Gabriel asked Holly.

'Always. I wish I could be more like her. She never lets anything get her down. No matter what happens, or how bad things get, she always manages to see the bright side.' Holly pointed to a table near the roaring fire on the left side of the pub and walked towards it. She hadn't meant to say that. Why couldn't she keep her mouth shut around this man? She shrugged off her coat. 'I'll get these to say thanks for helping with the decorations.'

'No you won't. You made me breakfast this morning, showed me how to deal with the Rayburn Dragon, baked the most delicious cupcakes and cooked me dinner. These are on me.'

There was no point in arguing. She could buy the next round.

'Thanks. I'll have a glass of red wine, please.'

'I'll get a bottle.'

Holly opened her mouth to say one glass was enough for her, but thought better of it. The night was young, and as Ivy would say, so was she.

Chapter Twelve

'What's the commotion out there?'

Holly had been chatting so intently with Gabriel that she hadn't noticed how late it was. It was only when people started to leave to make their way home that she glanced at her watch. It was gone eleven but instead of heading for their beds, several people seemed to have gathered outside the pub. She waved at Ivy to attract her attention.

'No idea,' Ivy said. 'Ned! What's going on?' She called out to Ned Stelling as he walked out of the door.

He shook his head. 'I'll find out.'

It only took him a few seconds. He came rushing back in, his face flushed and his eyes wide with excitement.

'You won't believe this,' he said. 'The pond has frozen over and so has Market Field. There're people skating on it…in their shoes, so sliding is more accurate. The Gaggle Gang's out there too.'

Suddenly, everyone in the pub stood up and hurried towards the door. Even Merlot and Mistletoe seemed to want to know what was going on. Merlot pushed past Holly, stuck her nose outside and bounded back in, obviously deciding it was too cold to find out. Mistletoe leapt across tables and chairs and sat on the farthest window sill, peering out. Holly nodded in her direction.

'The cat's got the right idea. It's absolutely freezing out there. I can feel it from in here.'

She and Gabriel were standing at the back of the crowd, having been the farthest away from the door. As they edged forward, it grew colder.

Holly stepped outside and the ground cracked beneath her feet. The grass on the bank had completely frozen over and the chestnut tree appeared to be made of ice. Even Holly's breath seemed to momentarily freeze in the air.

'Take my arm,' Gabriel said. 'It's a bit slippery.'

He was right about that. People were slipping and sliding all over the bank. The sensible ones made it to the wooden rail at the side of a flight of ice-covered, wooden steps which led down to the iced-over pathway that encircled the pond.

'I can't believe this,' Holly said, linking her arm through Gabriel's. She could feel him shivering.

That wasn't all she could feel. A sudden warmth shot through her body as if, just by being close to him, she was wrapped in a comforting blanket.

'Who, or what, is the Gaggle Gang?' Gabriel asked. 'Henry said something about geese earlier.'

'Can't you hear them?' Holly met his eyes and smiled.

Gabriel frowned and tipped his head to one side.

'That does sound like geese. Oh I see. It's a gaggle of geese. Do they visit the village when it's really cold? Is that what Henry meant about being able to tell it would be a cold winter because of the Gaggle Gang?'

Holly shook her head. 'Not exactly. It's a family of Embden geese and they're residents of Hideaway Down. They live in Meg Stanbridge's woodshed. Some people say that they can tell what the weather will be like depending on the behaviour of the geese.' She laughed. 'I don't think they've ever been right but one thing's for sure. You don't get in the way of the Gaggle Gang. They run this village like a gang of hoodlums in feathered coats.'

'I'm surprised they're out in such cold weather. I would've thought they'd want to be in the comparative warmth of the woodshed. I think Mistletoe had the right idea by staying inside.'

They made it as far as the top of the flight of wooden stairs and Holly looked up at Gabriel.

'Unless you want to go for a slide on the pond, I suggest we stay here and admire the view.'

And what a view it was. To a stranger's eye, it might have looked as if most of the village had turned out to try to catch a Christmas goose for their festive meal, and the geese, being none too bright, had got themselves caught in the centre of a frozen pond by their would-be assassins. Holly knew better. The Gaggle Gang, as always, took centre stage and chased away anyone foolish enough to come too close. Humans and geese alike were losing their footings and landing on their bottoms, feathered or otherwise.

'I'm not sure who's having the most fun,' Gabriel said. 'The geese or the people.'

Holly laughed. 'Neither do I, but I think the geese are the best skaters, by a feather.'

'Come on!' Ivy and Janet, having got their coats, grabbed Holly and Gabriel by their arms. 'This looks like fun.'

Holly and Gabriel exchanged doubtful glances but before they had time to object, they were dragged, slipping and sliding, onto the frozen crust of Hideaway pond.

Using the soles of their shoes as skates, they joined a higgledy-piggledy line with several others and skidded across the surface, trying to avoid those who fell in their paths.

Despite Holly's reservations, it was fun, and judging by Gabriel's throaty laughter, he thought so too.

The Snowdrop Inn looked magical, covered in a coating of frost, sparkling beneath the rows of multi-coloured fairy lights and surrounded by a sea of white. It resembled a scene from the perfect Christmas card, the ground frost creating an illusion of a light dusting of snow.

The lights from the pub, together with a solitary street lamp at the foot of the bank and the edge of the path, provided some illumination for the would-be skaters and the Arctic-like air was filled with laughter ringing out like church bells in the night.

'This is almost as good as ice skating at the Rockefeller Centre,' Ivy said, when they stopped for breath.

'If it's like this tomorrow,' said Ned Stelling, 'we should set up a makeshift rink. I'm sure some of the villagers have ice skates, and if not, we could probably hire some from somewhere.'

Ivy beamed at him. 'That's not a bad idea. And if we can't get skates, everyone can do what we've done and slide around in shoes.'

'Market Field is frozen solid,' Janet said. 'I know we were going to hold the Christmas Market in the church hall this year but wouldn't it be wonderful to hold it on a frozen field?'

'Are you mad, Mum?' Holly couldn't believe her ears. 'We can hardly stand up. How on earth would people shop on a field of ice?'

Janet shrugged. 'They managed it in the 18th century. You've read about the Frost Fairs on the River Thames in London. If they could do it, so can we.'

'That's true,' Gabriel said, clearly swept up by the unexpected turn of events. 'And Henry could probably provide some straw or something to scatter around to make walking less hazardous. It could be fun.'

Ivy gave him a playful nudge and caught his arm as he almost slipped over.

'I see you've found your spirit of adventure.'

'And I see you're still trying to kill me.'

72

'A Christmas market on ice would definitely be fun,' Holly said. 'And it would give the whole thing a far more festive feel than the church hall would. Plus in the field, unlike the River Thames, there's no danger of anyone drowning if they should fall through a patch of thin ice.'

'I'll call Kev the Rev right now,' Janet said. 'Give me your mobile, Holly. Mine's indoors.'

'So's mine. I left my bag inside. Besides, you can't call him at this time of night. It must be at least half-past-eleven. He's probably in bed.'

'He's a vicar. Vicars, like all emergency services, are on call twenty-four-seven. Does anyone have a phone?'

'Use mine.'

Gabriel handed Janet his iPhone and she made the call.

Holly looked on and shook her head. 'Speaking of eleven-thirty, I think it's time I went home to bed. I hadn't planned to stay this late and I've got lots of breakfasts to cook tomorrow.'

'At least you'll have a lift back up the hill,' Ivy said. 'I'll just help Mum close up and we'll be on our way. Bet you can't wait, huh?'

She slapped Gabriel playfully on his arm but this time, Holly caught him as he slipped.

'My entire body's tingling at the prospect,' he said, having regained his balance.

Holly grinned. 'I think that's more likely to be frostbite.'

Gabriel nodded, his grin as broad as Holly's and crossed his body with his arms, tucking his hands inside his sleeves.

'I think you're right. I really must get some gloves at this Christmas Market tomorrow.'

'Don't you mean at the Hideaway Down Frost Fair and Christmas Market?' Ivy said. 'What did Kev the Rev say, Mum?'

Janet handed Gabriel his phone. 'That he thought it was

73

an excellent idea. He's coming down first thing tomorrow and if it's still frozen, he'll help me make some calls. I'll get Gramps to help too. He was fast asleep in an armchair when we came out but he'll love it. The vendors will need to arrive earlier than planned if we're to set things up on a frozen field.'

'So it's really going to happen?' Gabriel asked. 'I can't quite believe it.'

Janet winked at him. 'You'll soon find out that anything can happen in Hideaway Down.'

'That I do believe,' Gabriel said.

Holly met his eyes. Why was he looking at her?

'I'll meet you two at the car,' Ivy said. 'I'll only be a couple of minutes.'

'Don't worry about helping me,' Janet said. 'It can wait until the morning. Just get your bag and head off home.'

'Thanks, Mum. I'll grab yours, Holly and meet you two at the car.'

With Ned Snelling's help, Ivy and Janet made it safely back to the pub, whilst Holly and Gabriel edged their way to the car park at the rear. Ivy joined them moments later and by eleven-forty-five, they arrived home, a little shaken after skidding up a black, ice-covered Hideaway Hill.

Holly wasn't in the least surprised when Gabriel insisted on helping them up the slippery path to the door of Holly Cottage but she was surprised by what was hanging above the door.

'Who put that up there?' She frowned at Ivy. 'That was you, wasn't it? When you said you'd forgotten something earlier. You came back to put this up, didn't you?'

'Guilty as charged.' Ivy beamed at her. 'And I'm going first. Come here Gabriel and give me a kiss.'

Gabriel blinked several times. The clichéd saying: 'Like a rabbit caught in the headlights' suited the expression on his face to perfection.

'Leave him alone, Ivy.'

'I would, but I can't. It's tradition. And we know how important tradition is at this time of year.'

She grabbed him by the collar, squeezed her eyes shut, puckered up her lips and with a loud, squelching sound effect, kissed him on the mouth. As quickly as she'd collared him, she let him go.

'Good night and pleasant dreams,' she said. 'Now it's Holly's turn. Make sure you do it, or you'll bring yourselves bad luck. And that's the last thing Holly needs right now.' With a parting grin, she dashed inside.

The last thing Holly needed right now was a sister meddling in her affairs... or to have to kiss a man who was occupying far more of her thoughts than she'd like.

'Ignore her,' she said, with a faint smile. 'And I apologise for her behaviour.'

'There's no need to apologise.'

Holly shrugged. 'Well, anyway... thanks for this evening. I had a really good time.'

'So did I. And it's me who should be thanking you. I was dreading this Christmas but since coming here... I've started to look forward to it.'

Holly met his eyes. They were as dark and enticing as brandy-laced, hot chocolate.

'So have I... a little.'

He moved a step closer. 'We'd better do as Ivy says. We don't want to tempt fate.'

Holly swallowed down her panic. Or was it excitement? With all twelve of the drummers from the *Twelve Days of Christmas* pounding on her heart, she took a step closer to Gabriel. Now they were only millimetres apart.

He removed his hands from his pockets and placed them gently on her arms.

'You'll… your hands will freeze.'

'No they won't, Holly.'

His lips met hers in a soft, brief kiss. Before she had time to enjoy the sensation, he eased himself away and she opened her eyes.

'That was for the mistletoe and tradition,' he said, a rasping quality in his voice. 'This one's for me.'

He wrapped his arms around her and pulled her tightly to him, kissing her in a way she was sure she had never been kissed before.

When he finally released her, she knew her smile was as wide as his. Grabbing him by the collar, as Ivy had done before her, she pulled him back towards her.

'And this one's for me,' she said.

Chapter Thirteen

Sunday, 20th December

'That looked like some kiss last night,' Ivy said, her hands wrapped round her Christmassy mug of coffee. 'Or to be precise, I should say 'kisses'.'

Holly had only been up for a few minutes and she entered the kitchen and glowered at Ivy.

'Were you watching us?'

'Of course. Sit down and I'll make you some coffee. You look like you've been visited by the ghosts of Christmas past, present *and* future, and it's not even Christmas Eve. I expected you to be full of festive cheer this morning. What's wrong? You didn't look this miserable last night. In fact, you were positively glowing when I went to bed. I know you weren't having passionate sex all night. I'd have heard that through the walls. Unless of course you were in the sitting room... or here in the kitchen. Well come on, tell me.'

Holly slumped into the armchair in front of the Rayburn, leant her head back and closed her eyes.

'Ivy. My head is thumping. My mouth feels as if Mistletoe spent the night curled up in it. I've had hardly any sleep. And no, I didn't have sex, passionate or otherwise in here, the sitting room, or anywhere else. Please would you be quiet for just five minutes until I've had some coffee?'

'I won't say another word.'

She didn't. Possibly for the first time in her life, at least as far as Holly was aware, Ivy remained silent for an entire, blissful five minutes. She handed Holly a glass of water and some headache pills; made her a steaming mug of coffee; passed her a mince pie, and perched on the edge of a kitchen chair, watching her over the rim of her own coffee mug.

'Time's up,' she said. 'So tell me. Why the glum face?'

'I thought it was too good to last.' Holly breathed out a long, slow, meaningful sigh. 'I know you mean well, Ivy but pushing Gabriel onto me isn't going to work.'

'He didn't need any pushing last night. I've seen the way he looks at you. He likes you, Holly. And whether you're prepared to admit it or not, you like him. What's the problem?'

'The problem, dear sister, is I've had my heart smashed into a thousand pieces. It hasn't mended. I'm still in love with Paul. I admit I like Gabriel. But of those thousand pieces, nine hundred and ninety belong to Paul. That leaves ten for Gabriel. I can't rush from one relationship to another.'

Ivy banged her mug on the table. 'Sometimes, Holly Gilroy, I want to beat some sense into you. Paul left you for your best friend eleven months ago. Eleven, Holly. I hardly call this 'rushing'. You have got to get over it. I know you were together for a long time but be honest. The relationship wasn't going anywhere. It wasn't moving forward. You were more like best friends than lovers. Paul betrayed you. When are you going to see that for what it really is? You're not star-crossed lovers. And you're not destined to be together. You read too many of those Gabriella Mann romance novels. That's the real problem. You think you and Paul will have a happy ending. You won't. At least not together. Paul's a jerk. You're better off without him.'

Holly rubbed her forehead. 'Don't sugar-coat it, Ivy. Give it to me straight. And I'm not a complete idiot. I know the difference between real life and fiction. I read those books because I enjoy them, not because I expect my life to be like that.'

'I'm sorry. I don't know how to get through to you. Why won't you just give it a chance with Gabriel? See how things go. You might be surprised.'

'Now you sound like the one who's been reading too many romances. What's the point? Gabriel's a guest. He's here for the holidays and then he'll go home. We've known one another for a little over a day. Yes, we seem to like many of the same things. We get on. I'll admit I'm attracted to him and yes, for several minutes last night, I did forget about Paul. I did think there might be the slightest possibility that I could fall in love with someone else. But I can't do that, Ivy. Not yet.'

Ivy smiled. 'I'm not asking you to fall in love. I'm asking you to be honest with yourself about Paul. To see him and what he did, as the rest of us do. He dumped you with a note, Holly – a bloody note. Shake off the chains of all those past Christmases you spent with him. Make new memories this Christmas. The only one holding on to the past, is you. Let this Christmas be about your future. Just promise me you'll try, and I'll shut up.'

'Oh my God. If that's what it takes to shut you up, I promise. I promise I'll try. Is that my ears ringing from your lecture? Or is someone at the door?'

'Hallelujah!' Ivy jumped up. 'It's the bell. I'll get it.' She walked into the hall. 'It's either Harry, with the milk or Gabriel back for a repeat performance of last night which, by the way, I still want details of in spite of what you've said. Don't panic. It's only Harry.'

'Only Harry!' Holly heard Harry Goode's dulcet tones.

'And a Goode, good morning to you too.'

'I didn't mean it like that,' Ivy said. 'You know I love you, Harry. Bloody hell! It's cold again this morning. Have you done your rounds in the village yet? Is the pond still frozen over? And Market Field? We were all skating on it last night. Mum's hoping we can hold the Christmas Market there today.'

Holly joined them in the hallway.

'Goode, good morning, Holly. I heard about the skating. And the field. Kev the Rev and your mum have already been on the phone to me and Dad this morning so we went to look at the field, first thing. It was still dark of course but it's definitely frozen. Can't see any problem, especially not as it's cold enough to freeze the b... very cold today.' He grinned sheepishly and handed Ivy two pints of milk. 'I see your guests are early risers. Lights are on in all three cottages.'

Holly groaned. 'I'd better go and get showered and dressed. If they're all up, they'll all be wanting breakfast. My life is full of joy. Have a Goode, good day, Harry.'

'Same to you, Holly. I know he was my friend, but don't let Paul get you down. You'll still be here after he and that girl have been and gone. Everyone's on your side... apart from his mum and dad, but even they're apologising. So don't you worry.'

That wasn't as much comfort to Holly as Harry had no doubt hoped it would be.

'Thanks, Harry. That's good to know.'

Chapter Fourteen

Gabriel couldn't concentrate. He had hardly slept a wink last night. All he could think about was Holly and that kiss. Or kisses to be more precise. He hadn't meant to kiss her. He'd thought about it, of course, but he hadn't actually meant to do it. It was Ivy's fault. If she hadn't hung that mistletoe over Holly's door, it wouldn't have happened.

Who was he kidding? He had been wanting to kiss Holly almost from the moment they met... when she'd answered the door on Friday night in those dancing reindeer PJs and a ring of toothpaste around her mouth. Well, maybe not from that moment but certainly from the following morning when she'd licked that second trickle of toothpaste from her chin.

Was he feeling like this because he was alone in a cottage miles from home? From everyone and everything he knew. Was it because this was his first Christmas without his gran? Or the rest of his family?

Was it because, in some strange way, he was missing Bryony?

Or was it simply because, from the moment he had seen Holly Gilroy, all his worries, doubts and plans had seemed to melt away?

He had gone from dreading this Christmas to looking forward to it. From spending it alone, hunched over his laptop, to the possibility of spending it with new friends. That in itself was a little Christmas miracle.

But he had to be careful. Last night, Holly had kissed him with as much enthusiasm as he had kissed her.

Suddenly, she had pulled away, apologised and dashed indoors without another word. The sad fact was, Holly was still in love with her ex-boyfriend and the man was coming back today.

From everything Gabriel had heard, Paul had behaved appallingly. He had slept with her best friend behind Holly's back and, like a coward and a bastard, he had broken the news to Holly with a note. And yet for all of that, Holly still loved the man. That made her either a loyal and devoted lover, or a martyr and a fool. Neither of which, helped Gabriel's case.

But Holly's love for Paul wasn't Gabriel's only problem. There was Bryony. She could ruin all his plans. And she had threatened to do precisely that when he had left his house on Friday. Of course, he hadn't taken her seriously. It wasn't the first time she had used that threat. She had said exactly the same words when he had ended their relationship two months ago, and so far, she hadn't carried out her threat. It wasn't really in her best interest to do so but one thing he had learnt while dating her, was that he never quite knew what Bryony would do next.

The doorbell startled him and he raced to the door, half hoping it was Holly, half praying that it wasn't.

'A Goode, good morning to you. I'm Harry Goode, delivering fresh milk to your door.' Harry smiled. 'I don't usually ring the bell but you didn't leave the bottles out, or a note saying how much milk you wanted today.'

Gabriel returned his smile. 'Good morning, Harry. I'm Gabriel. Gabriel Hardwick. I've been lucky enough to spend time with your dad. Sorry about the bottles. I did read that in the welcome pack yesterday but it completely slipped my mind.'

'Yes, Dad told me. You're the author who got lost.' His smile grew wider. 'I expect you've heard that several times.

That's what it's like in a village. Word gets round. Don't worry about the bottles. Any time is fine. Would you like milk today?'

'Yes please. I've got a funny feeling I'll be needing copious amounts of caffeine today.'

'You're not the only one,' Harry replied, handing Gabriel two bottles of milk. 'From the look of Holly, she'll be needing the same. Not Ivy though. That girl is livelier than electricity.'

'Holly... didn't look well?' He mustn't appear too concerned.

Harry shrugged. 'I wouldn't say that. More tired-like. As if she didn't get much sleep. But then I don't suppose she would, given the circumstances.'

'Circumstances?'

'Yes. Surely Dad told you? Holly's ex-boyfriend is coming back for the holidays. And he's bringing his new girlfriend. Holly was really cut up about the break-up, and the thought of seeing him again after so long is probably both a blessing and a curse. We're all behind her. I told her that just now. Well, I'd better get on. Have a Goode, good day.'

Gabriel could imagine what Holly probably thought about that.

'Thanks. And you. How much do I owe you for the milk?'

'You pay on your last day. I'll give you a bill. Are you going to the Christmas Market? It's going to be a real treat this year.'

'Yes. I'm hoping to go with Holly... and a couple of the other guests.'

He didn't want Harry to think there something going on between Holly and he, or that might be the new greeting. Instead of: "You're the author who got lost", it would be: "You're the author with the hots for Holly". Holly would find that about as amusing as he did, which was... not at all.

'Might see you there then,' Harry said.

He gave a final wave, walked down the path and made his way next door, where Gabriel saw three clean milk bottles waiting on the step with a little note tucked inside of one. They had clearly read their welcome pack.

Chapter Fifteen

'I'll get it,' Ivy called out from the hall, on her way back from the shower. 'But as Harry's already delivered the milk, there's only one person I can think of who would be ringing your doorbell at seven-thirty on a Sunday morning.'

'Not necessarily.'

Holly calmed the butterflies in her tummy as best she could and tucked the latest Gabriella Mann romance she had been reading, under the cushion of the kitchen armchair. In spite of Ivy's earlier comment, she would continue to read and enjoy the light-hearted books by one of her favourite authors; she would just make sure Ivy didn't see her do it for the next couple of days. One lecture from her sister was more than enough.

'Hello, Gabriel,' she heard Ivy say, in a cheery tone. 'What brings you here this morning? No heat? No breakfast? No idea? Don't look at me like that. I'm teasing you. Come in. Holly's in the kitchen.'

'Good morning, Ivy.' Holly heard Gabriel laugh. 'I came to say that I've had breakfast, and to see if I could help with anything.'

'Aren't you supposed to be writing a book?'

'That's what I keep telling myself. Unfortunately, it seems I'm not listening.' He stopped in the kitchen doorway and smiled at Holly. 'Hello, Holly. How are you this morning? God! That was a bit of a tongue twister.'

'Speaking of tongue twisters—'

'Ivy!' Holly interrupted. 'Don't you have something to do? Hello Gabriel.'

85

'Other than cause mischief, you mean?' Ivy winked at Gabriel. 'As it happens I do. Mum called me to ask if I'll go and help out as soon as I can. They're going ahead with a makeshift ice rink on the pond, and the Christmas Market's being held in Market Field. Or should that be 'on' as it's a block of ice, several inches deep? She asked if you'd help out too, once you've finished up here.'

'Oh, okay. Tell her I'll be there as soon as I can.'

'I'm happy to help,' Gabriel offered. 'If there's anything I can do.'

'I expect there're a lot of things you can do.' Ivy looked him up and down and grinned wickedly. 'Thanks. I'll tell Mum you'll be coming down with Holly later. Right. I'm off. Missing you already.'

Holly shook her head and got up from the armchair as Ivy skipped along the hall, singing *Oh Come All Ye Faithful.*

'Would you like a coffee? I was going to make some anyway.'

'Yes, please. She certainly knows her carols. And she's got a good voice. I haven't heard you sing any. Don't you like singing?'

Holly backed away as Gabriel walked towards her.

'I suppose you have to be cheerful to sing carols, and I haven't been feeling very cheerful.'

'You were cheerful last night.'

'Yes. Um. About last night. Please don't read anything into what happened on the doorstep. I'd had quite a lot to drink, what with the mulled wine here, followed by several glasses of wine at the pub. I think I was a bit… merry.'

She saw the look of disappointment sweep across his face and his dark eyes narrowed momentarily.

'I see. That's a shame. I rather enjoyed it and was hoping we might repeat it. But if you'd rather not, I hope

86

we can still be friends. I like you, Holly. I like spending time with you. I enjoy your company. I hope a few kisses under the mistletoe won't spoil that.'

She should be relieved. He had handled it magnanimously. Had she really wanted him to stride across the floor, sweep her up in his arms and kiss her passionately into submission? Perhaps Ivy was right. Perhaps she had read too many Gabriella Mann romances.

'No. No, of course not. They won't spoil it, I mean. I enjoy your company too. I'd like it if we could be friends.'

'Great. Friends it is.' He sounded as disappointed. 'It's freezing out there again today. I must remember to buy some gloves at the Christmas Market.'

'I'll remind you. Sit by the Rayburn and get warm. Is your cottage warm enough today?'

He smiled and walked towards the armchair. 'Yes. But as I had other things on my mind I nearly forgot to refuel it last night. I was so... um... Anyway, I eventually remembered. I think it's simply a matter of getting into the habit of doing it. You know, refuel Rayburn, switch off lights, clean teeth. That sort of thing.'

What had he been about to say? Other things on his mind? Had he been thinking about her? About their kisses? She had thought of little else all night.

'Yes. I do it automatically without even thinking about it.'

She made the coffee, remembering Gabriel took sugar in his, and turned around to place them on the table.

Oh dear God. He had found her book. He was staring at it as if he didn't quite believe his eyes. She sucked in a breath. Was he a book snob?

He raised his eyes to hers. 'Is this yours?'

'No. It's Ivy's. Would you like a mince pie?'

She turned away to get the tin but turned back, pulling

out a chair and dropping down onto it with a heavy heart.

'That's a lie. I don't know why I said that. The book's not Ivy's. It's mine. Gabriella Mann is one of my favourite authors and has been for many years. I've read every single one of her books. The most recent ones more than once. And this book is her best so far. There. I've said it.'

'You sound as if you're at one of those addiction groups, confessing to something you're ashamed of. Are you ashamed to read these books? Is that why you hid this one? Or… was there some other reason?'

He seemed cross. He clearly had a low opinion of romance novels and those who read them. How dare he? Millions of people the world over derived great pleasure from reading them. Who was he to stand in judgement?

'I'm not ashamed in the least. I know some people think it's easy to write a romance novel, but it isn't, you know. I've tried. Gabriella Mann is a superb writer and her characters jump out of the page. She makes you feel part of the story. As if you were there with the characters experiencing what they're experiencing. Laughing when they laugh, crying when they cry. Wanting them to find their happy ever after. Don't laugh at me!'

Gabriel shook his head. 'I wasn't laughing, believe me. I was smiling. You tried to write a romance novel? When? Recently?'

'After… after Paul left. I thought it might be cathartic. It wasn't. It was frustrating and humiliating.'

'I understand the frustration but why humiliating? Did you send it off to someone? Did you get a rejection? '

'No. I didn't even finish it. That's why it was humiliating. I've got an English Literature degree and I've worked in a bookshop since leaving university. I thought I could do it but I couldn't.'

'That's no reason to feel humiliated. Not everyone can

write a book. It certainly doesn't make you a failure.'

'I know. It was just the way I was feeling at the time.'

'That I understand. So... if you're not ashamed of reading this, why was it hidden behind the cushion? Why didn't you want me to see it?'

Holly laughed. 'I wasn't hiding it from you. I was hiding it from Ivy.'

'Ivy? Is she a romance novel-hater?'

'No. But she does think I read too many of them and that I expect my life to be like the heroines I read about. And before you ask, I don't. I know real life isn't like fiction. I know we can't all have a happy ever after.'

'I disagree with that. I think we *can* all have a happy ever after. It just depends how much we want it and where we look for it. Sometimes love is where we least expect to find it. My grandmother taught me that.'

He stared at the cover for a moment and ran his fingers over the embossed lettering of the author's name, Gabriella Mann. His head suddenly shot up and he met Holly's eyes.

'Sorry,' he continued. 'I like the feel of the cover.' He stood up and placed the book back behind the cushion before smiling at Holly. 'In case Ivy returns unexpectedly. So anyway, how can I help you this morning? Are you making breakfast for the other guests?'

That was all very odd. She hadn't expected that reaction at all.

'No. When Harry delivered their milk this morning there were notes outside both cottages. Basically, they're happy to fend for themselves. Harry popped back and told us. That means all I have to do is a bit of cleaning up and then I can go and help Mum and Ivy. I don't think there's anything you can help me with, to be honest. It's quicker if I do it myself. Thanks anyway.'

'In that case, I think I'll go and do some writing. I've

89

had a sudden flash of inspiration. Will you give me a shout when you're ready to go to the village?'

'Yes, of course. It'll be around nine.'

'Perfect,' he said. 'I'll see you later.'

Did his dark eyes linger on the cushion hiding the book as he left? Or had she just imagined that?

Chapter Sixteen

Holly couldn't help but smile at the expression on everyone's faces as she arrived at The Snowdrop Inn in Gabriel's gleaming red Jaguar. So this was how it felt to arrive somewhere in style? She could get used to this. Except she couldn't. Gabriel would be leaving after the holidays and she'd probably never see him again.

She should take a leaf from her sister's book and learn to enjoy the moment. Could she do that? Hadn't Ivy told her that the only person holding on to the past was her? That she should let this Christmas be about her future. But had she already ruined that? She'd told Gabriel not to read anything into last night's kisses. Now he seemed happy with merely being friends.

Gabriel got out and opened the passenger door for her. He even held out his hand to help her out. Not that she needed any help but she took it anyway.

'Gloves,' she said. 'You must remember to buy some gloves.'

He smiled. 'Remind me again later, please. I seem to have a memory like a sieve at the moment. I couldn't even remember the name of my main protagonist this morning, in the book I'm working on.'

'What is the book? I mean which genre?'

'A thriller. And this one's the first under my own name.'

'Gosh. That is *thrilling*. No more ghostwriting?'

He smiled. 'Not if everything goes to plan. We'll have to wait and see.'

'Come on you two!' Ivy yelled from the doorway of the

pub. 'Mum needs a hand in the kitchen, Holly. She says that she may be the best pub chef in the village but she's not a miracle worker.'

Holly laughed. 'Mum's the *only* pub chef in the village. Okay, I'm coming. What does she want Gabriel to do?'

Ivy shrugged. 'She said that she can't possibly ask one of the holiday guests to help out. But that if he's offering and doesn't have anything better to do, Kev the Rev could use some help in Market Field. Oh, and she said Gabriel could have a free lunch.'

'That seems fair,' Gabriel said. 'I'd better get myself to Market Field. See you at lunch.'

'Who put the grit and straw on the path?' Holly made her way over it from the pavement to the door of the pub. 'And more importantly, why didn't anyone think of it last night?'

'Harry and Henry did it this morning. Before the sun was up, Mum said.'

Holly glanced up at leaden skies. 'When did the sun come up? I must've missed that. I haven't seen a sign of it so far today.'

'I didn't mean it literally. It's probably a good thing there's no sun. The ice might melt and then we wouldn't have the ice rink or the Hideaway Down Christmas Market and Frost Fair.'

'No. But everyone would be in the church hall in the warm instead of freezing to death on an equally frozen field.'

Holly followed Ivy through the pub and into the kitchen.

'Finally,' Janet said. 'I'm so behind this morning, Holly darling, I don't know if I'm coming or going. Would you make pastry? Savoury for the various meat pies and sweet for the puddings. I haven't made a start on any of them yet. The meat and veg. are prepped so if you make the pastry,

Ivy can make the pies. Try not to put the Steak and Red Wine in the sweet pastry, Ivy, or the Caramel Apple in the savoury.'

'It might start a new trend,' Ivy said.

'Let's not experiment during Christmas week.' Janet searched frantically around her. 'Where did I put my glasses?'

'They're on your head, Mum,' Holly said.

'I knew I'd put them somewhere safe.'

They spent the next hour and a half baking, cooking and washing dishes… with the aid of a commercial dishwasher – but it did have to be loaded and unloaded. They made pies, both sweet and savoury; puddings and cakes; sauces and gravy; roast potatoes, boiled potatoes, mashed potatoes and chips. Roasted beef, turkey and pork were prepared, together with starters and desserts, including whipped cream and ice cream, custard and brandy sauce. Holly was almost dead on her feet by the time the pub opened at eleven a.m., sharp. Managing a bookshop had never been this tiring despite the long hours she had constantly put in.

She sank into a chair beside the fire with a cup of coffee and a mince pie and peered through the window overlooking the makeshift ice rink and the Christmas Market-cum-Frost Fair. Both of them had been open for about an hour, and both of them were packed. There was even a queue for the ice rink.

Jarvis Pope was sitting in a wooden hut the size of a sentry box, with a wooden pail at his feet and was charging a pound for people to slide around on a frozen pond. The money was going to charity, but even so, Holly couldn't quite believe it. But as her mum always said: "Anything can happen in Hideaway Down."

And last night, hadn't they all had a wonderful time doing exactly what these people were queueing up to do now? Holly would have willingly paid a pound for last night's fun and laughter. In fact, she would put a pound in the pail today.

'It sounds like they're all having fun,' Ivy said, joining her.

Janet wasn't far behind. She flopped down into the chair beside Holly and smiled at both of her daughters.

'There's nothing like the sound of children's laughter,' Janet said. 'Especially at this time of year. It reminds us all that life should be lived through the eyes of a child. Look at the wonderment in their little faces. Their bright eyes and rosy cheeks. Their innocent smiles and heartfelt joy. You two were like that once.'

'Ivy still is,' Holly said, grinning at her sister.

'And I hope I always will be. Life should also be lived to the full. Every moment is a gift. We shouldn't worry about what tomorrow may bring. That stops us from enjoying today.'

'Dear me,' Janet said, smiling. 'When did you get so profound?'

'I think it was after lugging that last keg of beer up from the cellar just now and worrying about whether my back would ache tomorrow.'

'You should've asked one of the men to do it,' Janet said.

'Speaking of men, I haven't seen Gabriel since he dropped me outside and went to help in Market Field. I wonder if I should go and check that he's okay.'

'Why do you care?' Ivy asked. 'You told me you're not interested in him.'

'No I didn't. Not that I am, but I didn't exactly say I wasn't.'

'What's this?' Janet leant forward, scanning each of her daughter's faces.

94

'It was pretty obvious to me that Gabriel was interested in Holly. I tried to help things along by hanging mistletoe outside the cottage door.'

'Gabriel! Gosh. And did it work?'

'If you mean, did he kiss me? Well, he didn't exactly have much choice. Ivy told him that it was bad luck not to and that I couldn't cope with any more of that. He could hardly walk away, could he?'

'I suppose not,' Janet said. 'Was it just a peck? Or was it a smacker on the lips?'

Ivy beamed. 'The first one was a peck.'

'The first one? You mean there were more? Holly! Why didn't you tell me, darling?'

Holly tutted. 'Because they didn't mean anything. I'd had too much to drink and so had he. It was just one of those silly Christmassy things. Like when you make out with someone at an office Christmas party and then realise the next day that you've made a mistake.'

'Are you saying you made out with him?'

'No, Mum. I'm saying I shouldn't have kissed him.'

'The third time,' Ivy added.

'The third time? You shouldn't have kissed him… three times? Well, you must've enjoyed it, darling.'

'I did enjoy it. I enjoyed it very much. But that's not the point.'

'What is then? And please don't tell me your hesitation has anything to do with that git, Paul Best.'

'It doesn't.'

Ivy glared at her. 'You told me it did.'

'Yes, well I thought it did. But really it has more to do with the fact that Gabriel's only here for the holidays. He'll go home and I'll never see him again. I'm still not over Paul – and there's no point in either of you giving me those looks. I'm not, and that's the truth. So the last thing I want to do is fall for someone else and get my heart broken all over again.'

'I can understand the last part, darling. But... what makes you think that Gabriel will break your heart? Yes, he's here for the holidays, and yes he'll go home afterwards. But as for never seeing him again... Well, Surrey may be another county but the last time I looked, it's less than a two-hour drive away.'

'I think we are all getting way ahead of ourselves,' Ivy said. 'Why don't you just loosen up, Holly and go with the flow? Wait and see what happens. Have some fun.'

Holly looked out towards the Christmas Market.

'I think I may just do that.'

'That's the spirit, darling. Good for you. But would you help me with the lunchtime rush first, please? A great many of those people having fun out there at the moment are going to be in here having fun, some time within the next half hour.'

'And one of those will be Gabriel,' Ivy said. 'Although he may not be having fun at the moment. I suppose that depends on what Kev the Rev has got him doing.'

'And he had better not be the only one getting a free lunch.' Holly got to her feet and stretched.

'Of course not, darling. But as Gramps always says: "There's no such thing as a free lunch."'

'Where is Gramps?' Holly asked. 'I haven't seen him all morning.'

'Kev the Rev roped him into playing the role of Father Christmas for the Santa's Grotto hut.' Janet stood up and linked her arm through Holly's. 'The last vicar always did it, as you know, but the new one felt that Gramps looked more the part. Gramps moaned about it of course, but as you can imagine, he was thrilled to be asked and I'm sure he's performing his role with gusto.'

'And with Merlot,' Ivy said. 'He took her with him and insisted they find an elf's hat and jacket for her. I must go down and take some photos later. I can't wait to post those on all my social media sites.'

'I think Mistletoe was worried that he'd do the same to her. She shot upstairs at the mention of the elf outfit and we haven't seen her since.'

'I don't blame her,' Holly said. 'I'd do the same if I thought someone might do that to me.'

'Ah,' Janet said, leading her daughters back towards the kitchen. 'It's funny you should mention that, darling.'

'Mum? No Mum. Absolutely not. No way. I am *not* dressing up as an elf.'

Chapter Seventeen

Gabriel was exhausted. He wasn't used to manual labour and he'd been doing nothing else for the last three hours. But he had to admit it was worth it.

The Christmas Market could hold its own against one of its European counterparts with the flat-pack, wooden chalets, where local traders sold their products, standing on a bed of ice.

Gabriel had helped erect those wooden chalets. He had also helped lug the bales of straw and bags of grit which had been scattered liberally along the thoroughfares between each row of chalets. He'd also helped with that, making sure there was enough of the frosty white surface visible under foot, to give the illusion of a dusting of snow.

He had helped various vendors carry boxes of their products to their particular chalets; helped hang myriad strings of multi-coloured fairy lights over and between each of the chalets.

He had even helped find an elf costume suitable for Janet Gilroy's Red Setter, Merlot and helped Gramps persuade Merlot to wear it. Once the dog had got it on, she seemed only too happy to play her part and Gabriel had taken several photos of her sitting proudly beside Gramps, who was dressed as Father Christmas.

If Janet Gilroy had told him two months ago when he'd booked Ivy Cottage, that he would be spending the Sunday morning before Christmas like this, he would have either gone to the Alps with his father, or jumped on a plane to Hawaii with his sister. Either would have seemed preferable. And yet he couldn't remember the last time he had had so much fun or felt so good. With the exception of last night, of course.

When Kev the Rev suggested it was time that Gabriel and some of the other helpers went to lunch, Gabriel wasn't sure what he was looking forward to most. Sitting down with a hot meal, or telling Holly about his morning.

He walked into The Snowdrop Inn with a huge smile on his face but as soon as he spotted Holly, he burst out laughing.

'Don't say a word,' she said. 'Not one word.'

Gabriel shook his head. He couldn't. He was laughing too much. He couldn't even tell her what he wanted for lunch when she asked, or what he wanted to drink. It was only when she threatened to throw a pint of beer over him that he managed to subdue his merriment.

'I'll have a pint of beer, please but in a glass, not over my head. You look as though you could use a drink, so get one for your elf.' He simply couldn't resist it.

'Ho, bloody Ho,' Holly said, pulling him a pint. 'I'm going to make Mum pay for this, that much you can count on. If she hadn't told me we were dressing up for charity, there would be no way she would've got me to wear this.'

'You should see Merlot,' Gabriel said. 'In fact you can. I took some pictures on my phone.'

He pulled out his iPhone and, when Holly placed the pint of beer in front of him, he showed her the pictures.

'Poor Merlot. She does look sweet though.'

'So do you.'

He met Holly's eyes. Even beneath the red face paint, he could see she was blushing.

'I look demented. I can't wait to get these clothes off.'

Now Gabriel had a sudden rush of heat. And not just to his cheeks.

'If you need a hand with that, I'm more than happy to help.'

Holly's eyelashes flickered and she quickly looked away.

'Here's the lunch menu. I'll come back when you've decided what you want.'

He almost said that he knew exactly what he wanted. But it wasn't on the menu.

'Hello lad.' Henry Goode tapped him on the shoulder.

'Hello Henry. How're you today? And who is this beautiful lady on your arm? I didn't know you had a daughter.'

'Cheeky monkey. This is Beth, my wife.'

'I'm very pleased to meet you, Beth. I'm Gabriel. The author who got lost on Friday night. Your husband's a lucky man to have such a stunning wife.'

Beth smiled at Gabriel, a delicate rose hue creeping across her peaches and cream complexion. Gabriel wasn't exaggerating. Beth was stunning. She might be wearing a few more laughter lines than she would probably like, but her beauty shone through.

'Thank you Gabriel,' she said, her voice as smooth as silk. 'I hear you've been seconded into helping out. I don't suppose this was how you expected to be spending your holiday.' She smiled up at him. 'Are you wishing now that Henry had pointed you in the wrong direction?'

'No. Bumping into Henry was a welcome start to what is rapidly turning into a rather special holiday. May I buy you both a drink?'

Henry shook his head. 'Thanks for the offer but we only popped in for a glass of Janet's mulled wine to warm us up before venturing around the Christmas Market. I saw you come in and wanted to say hello.'

'I'm glad you did. There's mulled wine at one of the

chalets, in case you need another. It's extremely cold out there.'

Beth nodded. 'But there's 'mulled wine' and 'musty-tasting mulled wine'. If you're planning on having some, I would recommend you come in here.'

'Good to know, thanks. Enjoy yourselves.'

'And you, lad.'

'Bye Beth, bye Harry.' Holly waved at them and glanced at Gabriel.

'Have you decided yet?'

'Yes. I'll have the Steak and Red Wine pie, please with sweet potato mash and honey glazed carrots.'

'On its way.'

'Holly. If you're free this afternoon, would you like to walk around the Christmas Market with me?'

She glanced towards Ivy, who was busy chatting to Ned.

'Um. I've got to nip into the church hall for a while and then go back to the cottages to make afternoon tea.'

'Oh. Okay, I'll give you a lift back, if you like. What time are you going?'

'About three. Um. If you'd like to go to the Christmas Market later, say about five-thirty, I'd be happy to go with you then.'

'You would?'

Holly nodded. 'I would. It should be really pretty later. Not that it isn't pretty now of course, but once it gets dark, the lights come into their own. There's something magical about it. And this year with the frozen ground, the lights will reflect even more. Did you remember to get some gloves?'

'Damn. I knew there was something I meant to do.'

Holly laughed. 'Don't worry. I'll remind you later. I'll even help you choose them.'

Gabriel couldn't wait. When had he ever before, been

this excited about buying a pair of gloves?

Chapter Eighteen

Holly glanced up. Something had landed on her cheeks and lashes as she walked around the Christmas Market, her arm linked through Gabriel's, at his suggestion, in case she slipped.

'Is that… is that… snow?'

Small, white flakes floated down through the cold, evening air.

'It is!' Gabriel sounded as excited as a child. 'We got my gloves just in time.' He waved his hands in front of them, showing off his black, leather gloves. 'If the snow settles, we can build a snowman. Or have a snowball fight.'

'Or sit in the warm and watch it.' Holly laughed.

'Spoilsport.'

'Child.'

Gabriel grinned. 'I feel a bit like a child. I don't know what it is about this place but I'm beginning to get excited about Christmas, especially now that I've bought a tree and decorations. And those coloured lights should look wonderful on the tree and twined around the pine boughs. I don't think I've ever seen such perfect mistletoe either. It's packed with berries.'

Holly smiled. She was getting excited about Christmas too. Something she didn't think would happen this year. She and Gabriel had bought so many things that they had already made three trips back to the car to unload.

'Perhaps we should go and see Santa,' she said. 'Then I think we can safely say that we have visited every chalet here.'

'That's a great idea. And after that, would you like another spin around the ice rink? It's looking even prettier this evening with all the coloured lights around the edge. It's been going down a storm with all the visitors, I hear.'

Holly could see the happiness in Gabriel's eyes and he'd said that as if he were a local, not a visitor himself. How strange that he should feel like that after just two days. And what was even stranger was that many of the locals seemed to be treating him as if he were a resident of the village. They had bumped into several local people whilst walking around the wooden chalets of the Christmas Market and in addition to greeting Holly, they had all said hello to Gabriel by name.

'You're starting to sound as if you've lived here for years. How have you managed to get to know so many of the villagers in such a short space of time? You've clearly made an impression. As for getting on that ice rink a second time, I'm not sure I want to risk breaking my ankle but I would like to go and watch those adventurous enough to do so. Or should I say, foolish enough?'

Gabriel smiled. 'It's strange,' he said, an inflection of wonderment in his voice, 'but I do feel as if I've lived here for years. I feel as if... this will sound really weird... but I feel as if I've come home. I've made more friends in this village in the last two days than I have in the road I live in, in Surrey, in the entire time I've been there. And I've lived in the same road in Epsom for more than ten years. Everyone in Hideaway Down is so welcoming. I didn't know places like this still existed. You're very lucky to live here, Holly.'

Holly cleared her throat. Why had his words made her feel so emotional?

'I suppose I am. No. I know I am. When you live here it's easy to take it all for granted but I've never really wanted to live anywhere else. I'm not like Ivy in that way. I don't crave excitement or yearn for adventure. I like seeing new places and meeting new people, don't get me wrong. I love going on holidays abroad, but I've never wanted to move to London like Ivy. And I couldn't possibly imagine emigrating to Australia, as Paul wanted me…'

Damn it. Why had she said that? Why had she reminded herself of Paul when she was having such a good time? When would she ever get through at least one day without thinking about the man?

'He wanted you to move to Australia?' Gabriel sounded genuinely surprised. 'Is that where he and… is that where he went?'

Holly nodded. 'Is that where he and Naomi went, you mean? Yes. Paul had wanted to leave Hideaway Down for years. He said it was his dream to go and live in Australia. It was one of the few things we argued about. Well, that and my job. But they were one and the same thing really. In addition to not wanting to leave my family, I didn't want to leave my job. I loved it. I loved working there. You've got to see the irony in that. I'm sure Paul will if he finds out. And someone is bound to tell him.'

'So… you didn't love him enough to move to Australia? To follow his dreams?'

Holly stopped in her tracks and pulled her arm away from Gabriel's.

'You sound just like him. What about *my* dreams? What about what I wanted? Didn't that count? Doesn't that matter?'

'Whoa. I didn't mean it like that, Holly. It wasn't a criticism, it was a question. I thought you… I got the impression that you would do anything to be with him. Some people will, to be with the person they love. Some people will sacrifice everything.'

'Yes. And some people end up miserable. That sort of love only works in fiction. I know myself better than that. Things might be fine for the first few months. Possibly even the first few years. But the excitement would soon wear off. Australia is a wonderful place and I loved our holidays there. But I knew I didn't want to live there on a permanent basis. As much as I loved Paul, I knew that was too big a price to pay and that we would both end up being miserable.' Holly sighed. 'Besides, I prefer my Christmases cold. May we change the subject, please? I don't know why I brought his name up.'

'Of course. But may I ask just one last question, please?'

'It depends what it is.'

Gabriel took a deep breath. 'If you knew that. If you knew you and he didn't want the same things in life, why did you stay together? Why do you still love him?'

Holly stared into the distance. 'Because... because fifteen years is a long time. And although he said Australia was his dream. I didn't really believe him. I honestly thought it was a fantasy. Perhaps I didn't know him as well as I thought I did. Perhaps I was selfish.' She met Gabriel's eyes. 'But just because two people don't want the same things, it doesn't mean they can't love each other. Does it?'

Gabriel shook his head. 'I suppose not. But it does mean that unless one of them is prepared to compromise, or in this case, sacrifice their dreams, the relationship is doomed. And surely that sort of love is futile?'

Holly stared at him. How had the conversation taken such a depressing turn? One minute they'd been talking about Santa, snow and happy village life, the next about doomed relationships.

'Cheer up you two.' Ivy beamed at them, appearing from nowhere. 'You look as if someone's just died. In case you haven't noticed, it's snowing. Can you believe that?

And it's Christmas. The season to be jolly. The time to have fun.'

'Any time is time to have fun as far as you're concerned,' Holly said. 'And it's only a few flakes of snow. I don't suppose it'll last. It's years since we've had snow at Christmas.'

'Bah humbug. Wouldn't it be lovely to have a white Christmas?'

'You might not say that when your car won't make it up Hideaway Hill, Ivy, or if we get snowed in. Gramps said it happened once many years ago. The village was virtually cut off.'

'I wouldn't mind getting snowed in,' Gabriel said. 'Especially now that I know how to use the Rayburn.' He winked at Holly.

'I'm just nipping off to see Santa whilst there's a lull in the pub,' Ivy said. 'Want to come with me? Perhaps if both you and I ask him nicely, we'll get a white Christmas.'

'Actually,' Holly said. 'We were just about to go and see him. Weren't we, Gabriel?'

'We were. And as much as I would like to have a white Christmas, I had already decided what I'm going to ask him for.' He held out his arms. 'Ladies, let's go and see Santa.'

Holly and Ivy linked their arms through his and they wove their way towards the winter wonderland of Santa's Grotto where Gramps would be doing his thing.

Chapter Nineteen

Santa's Grotto was positioned in the centre of the Christmas Market. It was an open-fronted, wooden chalet painted red with white trimmings, with white felt wadding and cotton wool, for snow. The chalet was surrounded by Christmas trees, sprayed with fake snow and dripping with foil-covered, chocolate decorations, gingerbread men and candy canes.

Gnomes from Sarah Saltcote's garden were dressed up to look like elves and together with plastic reindeer, they lined the straw-covered path leading to the chair where Santa sat, with Merlot, Santa's Setter, sitting proudly by his side. They were flanked by two choirboys from St Catherine's Church, who had been appointed 'Elf and Safe-sweety Officers', with the responsibility of handing out either a gingerbread man or candy cane to every person leaving Santa's knee.

As Holly, Ivy and Gabriel waited in the queue, Ivy pointed out that for each treat the choirboy elves dished out, they took one for themselves.

'At least they had the decency to give a gingerbread man to Merlot a moment ago,' Holly said. 'Although what that may do to her tummy, I'm not so sure.'

'I think I'll have a quiet word with them when we collect our treats,' Ivy said. She looked Gabriel up and down. 'I hope Santa's knee can take your weight.'

Gabriel laughed. 'I hope you're not suggesting I'm overweight. I may not be as fit as I thought I was, but I do try to keep in shape. Actually, that's a lie. I don't.'

'I'm not suggesting any such thing. You look pretty fit

to me. In every sense of the word.' Ivy winked at him. 'But you're over six foot and "a strapping lad" as Gramps would say and Gramps is eighty-four, with creaking bones. Just don't break his leg.'

'I promise I'll be careful.'

'Good. You can go first.'

Ivy pushed Gabriel towards Gramps, who promptly jumped up, coaxed Gabriel into the red velvet, padded armchair he had vacated and sat on Gabriel's lap, to loud cheers and hoots of laughter.

'Well son,' Gramps said. 'What would you like for Christmas, or shall I guess? Does it begin with the letter H and end with a kiss under the mistletoe?'

'How did you know that?'

'I'm Santa. Santa knows everything. So I'm right?'

Gabriel nodded.

'I'll see what I can do. But you've got to promise me one thing. Whatever happens, you won't break her heart and you definitely won't end things by leaving her a note. Holly's not just for Christmas, she's for life, so be careful what you wish for or next year you'll be on more than Santa's naughty list. Got that?'

'Got it.'

'Want to change your mind and ask for something else?'

Gabriel shook his head. 'No. Holly's all I want for Christmas. I can't promise you she's for life but I can promise you she's not just for Christmas and that if things don't work out, I'll tell her to her face. Although if the way I feel now is anything to go by, she'll be the one who'll be doing the dumping. That's assuming she will even take me on.'

Gramps smiled at him. 'I've seen the way you look at one another. I was beginning to think I wouldn't live to see the day when Holly would get over Paul and fall for someone else. But I've seen a change in her these last two days and there's more than a glimmer of hope on the horizon. Now give me back my chair.'

Gabriel beamed and stood up. 'Merry Christmas, Santa.'

'Merry Christmas to you, Gabriel. Next!'

Gabriel took the candy cane offered by the elf and waited for Holly and Ivy. Holly had been right about the snow. It had only lasted for five minutes.

Holly kissed her grandad on the cheek and perched on the edge of the chair. If only he could hear what she wanted for Christmas. She and Gramps were looking in his direction. Had Gramps told her what he had asked for? Would Santa do that? Or was she telling him she'd like Paul back?

He'd soon find out because she was heading his way. That was quick. At least she was smiling.

'What did you ask Santa for?' Gabriel asked.

'That would be telling. I wonder what Ivy's asking for. She told me she's got her eye on someone but she's being unusually coy. She won't tell me who it is.'

'Could it be Ned Stelling?'

'Ned? No way. Ned's a blacksmith.'

'Er. Does Ivy have something against blacksmiths?'

'Of course not.'

'Then I don't follow you. What's his occupation got to do with it?'

'Ivy loves living in London. You don't see many blacksmiths in London. Besides, Ned loves Hideaway Down as much as I do. Maybe even more. His family have lived here for generations. He'll never leave the place. It would be like me and Paul all over again.'

Gabriel fought back a chuckle. Holly was being serious.

'It's not quite the same thing, Holly. London is hardly Australia. It's less than a two-hour drive away. Unless you get lost.'

'I suppose you're right. But Ned and Ivy?' Holly shook her head. 'That I didn't see coming. What makes you think it's him?'

Gabriel shrugged. 'The way they behave when they're together. I've seen them talking a few times and there's just something about it. And last night, on the makeshift ice rink... I don't know. He seemed to be taking extra special care of her. I could be on completely the wrong track, of course.'

Holly's brows furrowed and she stared at Ivy.

'They've been friends for years. We all have. But now that you come to mention it, there may be something in what you say. That would be a turn-up for the books. I'd love it to be true. It would be wonderful to have her here more often. And Ned is one of the nicest guys I know. But that's me being selfish again.'

'Loving your sister and wanting to see more of her isn't being selfish, Holly. And you want her to be happy.'

Holly smiled up at him. 'D'you fancy going for a quick drink in the pub? Ivy's working there tonight and, if it's true about her and Ned, he'll be in there too.'

'Spy on them you mean? Is that really fair?'

'Not exactly spy. Just... see if there's anything in it.'

'Couldn't you just ask her?'

'I could. But unless she's really fallen for him, she wouldn't tell me. Ivy believes in having fun so she'd probably say that's all it is. If she is serious about him, really serious, she'll tell me when she's ready.'

'Then why not wait until she's ready?'

Holly shrugged. 'I suppose I could.' She kicked a piece of straw with the toe of her boot. 'Don't you... don't you want to go for a drink?'

'I'd love to. But won't you get roped in to help behind

the bar? It's probably going to be packed in there.'

'It will be. But Mum won't ask me to work there tonight. Besides, it'll only be a quick drink. I didn't get much sleep last night. I could do with an early night.'

'You and me both. Okay then. One quick drink. But no spying.'

'Spoilsport.'

Gabriel smiled. 'Child.'

'Okay,' Ivy said. 'That's that sorted. We're going to have a white Christmas and I'm going to be made Queen of a small country in 2016. Plus, I've had a quiet word with the Elf and Safe-sweety Officers and I've told them there's to be no more embezzling of the Santa Company confectionery.'

'It looks like you took a bribe,' Gabriel quipped.

Ivy had four candy canes, three gingerbread men and two foil-wrapped chocolate decorations in her hand.

'That's known as Queen's bounty or something like that. Besides, it's a long walk back to the pub.'

'Yes,' Holly said. 'It's going to take all of ten minutes. Gabriel and I are popping in for a drink, by the way.'

'Tonight?' Ivy looked concerned.

'Yes. Any reason why you don't want us to?'

Ivy frowned. 'I wasn't thinking about me, Holly. I was thinking about you. Don't forget it's Sunday night.'

Holly laughed. 'I know what day it is.'

'Well then…?'

'What's the problem with Sunday night?' Gabriel asked.

'Oh.' Holly visibly stiffened. 'Because it's the night that Paul and Naomi are coming to Hideaway Down.'

112

Chapter Twenty

'Thank you for bringing me home, Gabriel,' Holly said. 'And for being so understanding.'

They were standing beneath the mistletoe, just like they had been last night. But this wasn't the time to reach out and kiss her. Even though that's exactly what he wanted to do. That, and wrap his arms around her and tell her that everything would be all right.

'I'm sorry I can do so little. Please tell me if there's anything I can do to help.'

Holly shook her head. 'Thanks. I appreciate that. But as Ivy told me the other day, the only person who can do anything about the way I feel, is me. Or words to that effect. I've got to face him sometime. I've got to accept them as a couple. Mum says she'll throw him in the pond if he comes into the pub. But that's not really fair. The Snowdrop Inn's the only pub in the village. Paul's parents live in the village. They go into the pub. Everyone likes them, including me. Why shouldn't Paul and Naomi be able to go there with his mum and dad? Especially at Christmas.'

'That's very forgiving of you. And if my opinion counts for anything, I think you're right. He should be able to go to the pub without fear of being stoned. Or thrown in the pond. Although, as it's currently frozen over... Sorry, I didn't mean to make light of the situation.'

Holly smiled up at him. 'To be honest, I think that's exactly what I need. Someone to make light of it. And to help me do the same. It's time I forgave him. Time I forgave them. Time I got on with living my life and planning my future. Not living in my past.'

Gabriel looked into her eyes. Did she really mean that?

'If there's anything I can do to help with that...'

Did she know what he meant? Was he making himself clear? How long could he stand here with her looking at him like that before he had to reach out and pull her to him? Should he just do it? Is that what she wanted?

'Thanks, Gabriel.' She finally looked away. 'All I want is a hot bath, something to eat and to curl up by the fire.'

'That sounds like the perfect evening. Look, I'm no chef or anything but I can make a mean Spaghetti Bolognese. Why don't you have a bath, throw on a tracksuit or something comfortable and join me for supper? It's seven-thirty now. Let's say eight-fifteen. I've got wine and everything we need. Come round when you're ready.'

He could see by the tiny line between her brows that she was having doubts.

'I don't want to put you to any trouble.'

'It's no trouble. I would offer to come in to yours, but I might outstay my welcome and you'd feel awkward asking me to leave. This way, you can leave whenever you want. Please say you'll come, Holly. You'd be doing me a favour. After such a lovely day, it would be an anti-climax if I had to eat alone. And you can tell me where to put the decorations. I'll do all the work. You can sit and supervise.'

The line disappeared from her face and she smiled.

'Thanks. I'd like that. I may even help. I'll see you at eight-fifteen.'

'If you can't decide what to wear, you looked pretty good in those dancing reindeer pyjamas. I just thought I would mention that. Oh shit! I didn't mean... that is, I wasn't suggesting we should... that I would... that we...'

She placed her finger over his lips and smiled.

'That's okay, Gabriel. I know you weren't suggesting

we jump into bed together.' She glanced up at the mistletoe and her eyes twinkled. 'Although if last night's kisses were anything to go by, that would be something to look forward to sometime in the not too distant future.'

What the hell…? Had she just said that she had enjoyed last night's kisses as much as he had? That the idea of going to bed with him wasn't completely out of the question?

Before he could get his head around it, she kissed him on the lips and dashed inside her cottage.

Chapter Twenty-One

Holly wiggled her toes beneath the lavender-scented bubbles and giggled. Taking a leaf out of Ivy's book was much more fun than she'd imagined. Had she actually just told Gabriel that she liked the thought of going to bed with him? Had she really behaved so brazenly?

The look on his face had been priceless. And when she'd kissed him, it was obvious his mind was working overtime. What would he be doing right now? What would he be thinking?

Tingles of excitement chased up and down her body like Christmas lights on a repeater program and she grinned at the pictures flicking through her mind. When was the last time she had felt such excitement? Such... longing. Longing? Was she really longing to go to bed with Gabriel?

How could that be possible? After everything she had said and felt about Paul. The reason she and Gabriel had left the village so early was because she didn't want to bump into Paul. Wasn't it?

Why then, was it Gabriel she wanted to kiss? Why did she want to feel Gabriel's arms around her? To look into Gabriel's eyes? To hear Gabriel's voice? See Gabriel's smile?

She must calm down.

She closed her eyes and lowered her head beneath the water, sliding her body further down the length of the bath until she was entirely submerged in a cocoon of warming lavender. She held her breath for as long as possible before rising to the surface with a smile.

Her phone was ringing but she ignored it.

It rang again.

And then again.

Someone clearly wanted to talk to her.

She glanced at the clock on the bathroom wall. It was seven-fifty-five. She had better get out and get ready. She didn't want to be late on her first date with Gabriel.

Was it a date? It felt like a date.

The phone rang again and she clambered out of the bath to answer it.

'Where the hell have you been?' Ivy screeched. 'I've been ringing you for the past five minutes. Is he there?'

'Is who there? I mean, here. I was in the bath. What's up, Ivy? Why are you sounding so annoyed?'

'Gabriel! Is Gabriel there?'

'No. But I'm going next door to have supper with him in about ten minutes. Do you want to speak to him? Shall I get him to call you?'

'Call me! No, I don't want him to bloody well call me.'

'What on earth's going on? What's the matter, Ivy? What's happened? Is something wrong? Has something happened to his dad?'

'What? No. But something's going to happen to him the minute I get my hands on him. In fact, he'll be lucky if I don't wring his neck '

'What? Ivy! For God's sake tell me. What is going on?'

'You said he's next door? And you're in your cottage?'

'Yes. With just a towel wrapped around me at the moment. If this is your idea of a joke, it's not very funny. Why do you want to wring his neck?'

'Because he's a bastard and a liar.'

Holly shivered but not entirely from cold.

'A what?'

'I don't want to tell you over the phone. Mum says she can manage, so I'm coming up. Stay there and wait for me.

Holly, are you listening? Just stay in the kitchen and wait for me. Don't answer the door. Don't answer the phone. Don't look out the window. Just sit in the kitchen and wait. I'll be there in five minutes. I'm getting in the car right now.'

Holly swallowed down the sick feeling in her throat.

'You're getting me worried, Ivy. Ivy? Ivy, are you there?'

Ivy had rung off.

Holly sat on the edge of the bath and stared at the tiles on the floor. What could Ivy be talking about? What could she have meant? She shivered again and in a trance-like state, pulled on her dressing gown, slid her feet into her slippers and padded downstairs to the kitchen.

She flopped into the armchair in front of the Rayburn and retrieved the Gabriella Mann romance from beneath the cushion, as it dug into her back. Cradling it in her arms, she waited for Ivy to arrive.

She heard a car pull up but it didn't sound like Ivy's. Ivy's car always screeched to a halt. This car purred. She got to her feet to look outside but Ivy had told her not to. She would do it anyway. Someone was walking up the path. Clip-clopping, to be precise. But not the path to Holly Cottage. Before she reached the window there was a screech of brakes. Ivy had arrived.

Seconds later, Ivy burst in through the front door.

'I told you not to look. Did you see?' Anger and concern drew lines on Ivy's face.

'What is going on?'

'Sit down and prepare yourself for a shock.'

Ivy grabbed a bottle of wine, opened it and filled two large glasses to the brim. She handed one to Holly and took three straight gulps from hers.

'Drink,' she demanded. 'You'll need it.'

Holly shook her head. 'Just tell me.'

Ivy took a deep breath. 'Gabriel has a girlfriend.'

Wine spilled onto Holly's lap but she ignored it. Ivy grabbed a tea towel and handed it to her.

'What do you mean? How can Gabriel have a girlfriend?'

'That's what everyone at the pub is asking.'

Holly shook her head and swiped away a solitary tear. 'But he can't have. He would've told me. He would've said something.'

'You'd think so, wouldn't you? That's what any decent guy would do. It seems our Gabriel isn't quite the angel he makes out. According to his girlfriend, who by the way, is also his agent, they've been together for two years. Or, to quote Bryony: "We've worked together for many years but we've been in a serious relationship for two. We simply couldn't deny our passion any longer."

'Bryony?'

'The girlfriend. Are you taking this in? Gabriel's been sleeping with his agent for the past two years.'

'But I don't understand. If that's the case, why did he come to Ivy Cottage on his own?'

'Because *Bryony* was busy negotiating film rights and another book deal on *his* behalf and *he* was supposed to be here writing his new book. She said she wanted to surprise him. I'll bloody surprise him. I've got a good mind to go round there right now and tell him exactly what I think of him. Mum is livid. No one can quite believe it.'

'Nor can I.'

Holly knocked back the remaining contents of her wine glass in several long gulps.

Chapter Twenty-Two

Since the moment Gabriel left Holly's door, all he could think about was her. Her lips, her eyes, her hair, her body. How would it feel to take her in his arms and know that he wouldn't have to let her go? It was up to her, of course. He would let her dictate the pace. He didn't want to rush her.

He brought in all his purchases from the car and counted down the minutes. Would she be late? Would she be early? He made the Bolognese sauce. He would put the pasta on the hob when she arrived. He fixed the Christmas tree into the stand he'd purchased and tried it in various positions around the sitting room, finally placing it in one corner near the wood burner – but not too near. He opened the wine and poured a glass, almost jumping out of his skin when the doorbell rang.

Eight o'clock. She was early. That was a good sign. He raced to the door. He didn't want to keep her waiting outside in the cold.

'Surprise!'

Gabriel blinked like a camera shutter at high speed.

'Bryony? Shit! Bryony! What the hell are you doing here?'

'And it's lovely to see you too, darling. Well, let me in. It's freezing out here.'

Gabriel pushed past her and peered towards Holly Cottage. There was no sign of Holly.

'How the hell did you get here?'

'I drove, darling. Let me in.'

'How did you find the place? It's in the middle of nowhere.'

'It's a country village, Gabriel. Not the hidden paradise of Shangri-La.'

She was wrong about that. That was exactly what it was. Or it had been, until she had shown up.

'But... how did you know I was here? I didn't tell you where I was going.'

Bryony tutted. 'I called your family.'

Gabriel sneered. 'I don't believe that. They wouldn't have told you.'

'Give me some credit, darling. I called your stepmother and told her I needed to contact you urgently. She gave me the details on the spot. Your father keeps her well-informed. Either that or she knows all his passwords. Anyway, what does that matter? I'm here now. But you're not being very civil. Are you really going to make me stand out here all night?'

'No Bryony, I'm not. You can get back in your car and go home.'

'Gabriel! That isn't very nice. I've driven a long way to see you. Besides, I have news. Exciting news. Believe me, darling, you'll want to hear it.'

'Then call me tomorrow and tell me.'

'But I'm here tonight. I'll tell you now.'

'I have plans tonight. I don't have time to listen. Please Bryony. Do us both a favour. Get in your car and go.'

'No, Gabriel! I won't. I'm tired. I'm hungry. I'm cold. And I need a decent glass of wine. The wine in that pub was so awful I had to have a G&T. And I'm trying to give up gin.'

'The pub? Which pub?'

'Apparently, there's only one in this godforsaken village. Don't you find the place sickeningly twee?'

'You went to the pub? The Snowdrop Inn?'

'What is wrong with your throat, darling? You sound

121

like a strangled mouse. Yes, I went to the pub. Traffic was bumper-to-bumper and my satnav kept pointing me in a different direction every time I turned a corner. I needed the loo, so I went to the pub. I asked if they knew you and lo and behold, they did.'

Gabriel leant against the wall for support and closed his eyes tight.

'Bryony. Please, please, please, tell me you didn't say you were my girlfriend.'

He opened his eyes and silently prayed.

'Well of course I did. I wanted to know where you were. I could hardly tell them I was your agent. I didn't know whether you were keeping that a secret. I know how funny you get about these things. Now really darling. It's time you let me in. Hollywood is calling. Figuratively speaking. Literally, they telephoned me yesterday.'

'Hollywood?'

'Uh-huh. I knew that would interest you. And more than one film studio. Pour us some wine and I'll tell you all about it.'

Gabriel shook his head and rubbed his temple with one hand.

'Bryony. I don't know how to say this in words you'll understand. So please listen very carefully. I don't want you here. I don't want to talk to you tonight. I'm not interested in anything to do with Hollywood at this precise moment in time. Please go home. I promise faithfully I will call you tomorrow and talk to you for hours if that's what it takes.'

'You're the one who doesn't understand. I'm talking about a movie deal, Gabriel. And not just one movie – a series. Do you know what that means? It means you can virtually write your own cheque.'

'I'll try again. Bryony. I. Don't. Care. Not tonight. Go.

122

Home.'

'Well, I do care, Gabriel. You may be willing to throw away everything we've worked for, but I'm not. Either you let me in, or I'm calling the tabloids right now. I'm serious this time.'

She pulled out her iPhone and dialled a number, pressing the speaker button and holding the phone at arm's-length.

Gabriel closed his eyes and stepped aside. 'Okay Bryony. You win. Turn off the phone and you can come in.'

'Thank you, darling. That's more like it. Oh. Where are you going?'

'There's wine on the table. Help yourself. I'm just going next door for a moment. There's something I need to do.'

'Don't be long. We've got lots to talk about.'

Gabriel closed the door behind him and ran to Holly Cottage. This could not be happening. This really couldn't be happening. At least he could explain to Holly. He rang the doorbell and waited.

And waited.

And waited.

He rang again.

And waited.

Why wasn't she answering? Was she still in the bath? The lights were on downstairs. He peered through the sitting-room window. No sign of her in there. He rang the bell again.

And waited.

Finally, the door swung open but it wasn't Holly standing in the doorway with a face like thunder. It was Ivy.

'Yes,' she hissed.

'Ivy! Um. Is everything all right? I need to talk to Holly. May I come in?'

'I don't know, Gabriel. *Is* everything all right? Holly doesn't want to talk to you. And neither do I, particularly. And no, you may *not* come in. In fact, you will never set foot in this cottage again. Do give our regards to Bryony. Then do us all a favour and jump off Hideaway Cliff.'

'Ivy! I can explain. It's not what you think. She's not my girlfriend. Bryony's not my girlfriend. She's my agent. Just my agent.'

'That's not what Bryony says. Perhaps you should be telling her, not me.'

The palm of his hand slapped against the closing door.

'Please Ivy. Please don't shut me out. Please let me explain. She was my girlfriend but it's over.'

'Again, tell her, not me.'

He pushed hard against the door to stop it shutting.

'I have told her. I've told her several times. She just doesn't want to hear it.'

'At the risk of repeating myself. Her. Not me. I don't care.'

'How can you believe I would do this? You know me.'

'We thought we did. But two days is hardly long enough to get to know the real person behind the façade. No wonder you write fiction. You spun a web of lies for us.'

'I didn't. I'm telling you the truth.'

'Tell someone who gives a damn. Now get your hand off our door or I'll call the police. Or better still, I'll call some of the villagers. They have one or two things they'd like to say to you.'

'How can you believe this?'

'Men lie, Gabriel. My dad. Paul. You. Men like you are all the same. You give the decent ones a bad name. Now I don't want to tell you again. Go. Away. You're not welcome here.'

'But...' He sounded like Bryony. Ivy was telling him to

go. He wasn't listening. 'Okay. I'll go. But please tell Holly, this isn't what she thinks. I haven't lied. I'm not lying now. Bryony is not my girlfriend.'

'Then perhaps she should tell us that.'

Would she? Of course she wouldn't. She'd say it was some kind of joke. His hand slid from the door. There was no point tonight. He'd have to try again tomorrow.

'I thought not,' Ivy said.

The slamming door was like a gun going off – its bullet went straight through his heart.

Chapter Twenty-Three

Holly sat at a corner table near the fire, at the end of the pub farthest from the pond. She didn't want to look out at it and recall her now equally frozen memories of the last few days. How ironic that she had hoped to hide away from heartbreak at the cottages and avoid the pub and now she was hiding in the pub to avoid the cottages. Ivy had offered to switch jobs. Ivy would cook and clean for the holiday guests; Holly would work at the pub. She'd just go home to sleep, although her mum had said both she and Ivy were welcome to stay at the pub.

Holly stared into the flames as the red foil garlands hanging nearby, swayed gently back and forth in the wafts of heat rising upwards from the hearth. Back and forth, back and forth, like the pendulum of a clock slowly ticking off the seconds of her misery.

'Here, my darling, drink this.'

Janet handed her a mug of brandy-laced, hot chocolate, topped with whipped cream and sprinkled with baby marshmallows, floating like tiny islands in a stormy sea.

'Thanks Mum.'

'He had us all fooled,' Janet said. 'I can't believe he did this to you. To us. To everyone in Hideaway Down.'

'Nor can I. And that's the problem. It doesn't make any sense. I mean, he didn't know us. He definitely didn't fall in love with me at first sight. So why the pretence? Why the charade? What did he hope to gain by it?'

'Sex, I suppose. It's always about sex with some men.'

'I don't know. He didn't seem that type. But don't worry, Mum. I'll get over it. And the good news is, meeting him showed me that, without even realising it, I'm over Paul. Don't look at me like that. I'm not exchanging one heartache for another. Even Ivy said it. I was clinging to the past. I couldn't get over Paul because I didn't want to get over him. I wouldn't let myself get over him. But if I still loved him, I wouldn't have felt the way I felt about... Gabriel. So he actually did me a favour. It just doesn't feel like it at the moment.'

Janet wiped a tear from her eye. 'You've got me all emotional, darling. I'm so proud of you. You and Ivy are the best girls in the world. The best daughters any mother could wish for. And you'll see, Holly. One day you'll meet a man who'll realise just how special you are. And he'll never let you go. And he'll never make you cry.'

Holly grinned. 'I'm reading about a man like that in the latest Gabriella Mann romance. I don't think they exist in real life, Mum. But I suppose it's nice to dream.'

'They do, darling. I know that may be hard to believe, especially at a time like this. Your dad left. Paul left. And now Gabriel has shown his true colours. But somewhere out there, Holly, is a man for each and every one of us. I believe that. A good man. I still think I'll get my happy ever after ending and I know here in my heart, that you and Ivy will. Now drink your hot chocolate before it gets cold. It's The Best Mince Pie contest today and we know how exciting that can be. We wouldn't want to miss that, would we?'

The last thing Holly felt like doing was dragging her sleep-deprived body to the church hall to watch The Best Mince Pie contest. Her mum meant well, Holly knew that but everyone in the village was already wondering how she would cope with seeing Paul and Naomi. Now they'd all be wondering how she would cope with having been tricked and lied to by Gabriel. She knew the news of Gabriel's girlfriend's arrival would have swept over the village last night faster than a snow storm.

She took several gulps of the hot chocolate and cradled the bowl-shaped mug to her chest. She would have to face the music sometime. It might as well be Christmas music at The Best Mince Pie contest. She glanced at her watch. Eleven-fifteen. What would Gabriel be doing now? More to the point, what would Gabriel and *his girlfriend* be doing now? He had already been back to Holly's cottage – twice – this morning, ringing her doorbell repeatedly and banging on the door for a good ten minutes. Ivy had shouted through the letterbox at him to go away.

'Holly doesn't want to see you,' Ivy had told him. 'And nor do I, you lump of reindeer poo. How many more times do I have to tell you? We're not interested in your excuses and feeble explanations. Go back to your girlfriend. And by the way, you can do your own bloody cooking and cleaning and if you don't like it, you can bugger off back to Surrey. Mum says she'll even give you a refund for the remainder of your stay, if that will encourage you to go.'

'I'm not going anywhere until I've spoken to Holly,' Gabriel had replied. 'And I'm going to keep ringing this bell and banging on this door every hour until she'll see me.'

'Fine. But we're not going to let you in. If you choose to freeze to death out there, be our guest.'

Ivy had turned the radio up in the kitchen to let the Christmas carols drown out Gabriel's pleas. The continued ringing of the bell and banging on the door had sounded like some sort of musical accompaniment.

It was Ivy's suggestion that Holly should go down to

128

The Snowdrop Inn.

'At least if Gabriel tries to see you there, some of the villagers will send him on his way,' she'd said.

'I don't understand why he's being so persistent,' Holly had told her. 'I mean, what could he possibly say? The game's up. Everyone knows he's got a girlfriend. Why doesn't he just let it go? And what must she be feeling? How humiliating must it be to turn up on your boyfriend's doorstep, unannounced, only to find out he's been trying to seduce another woman? And then to find that same boyfriend keeps popping to the other woman's house to try to spin her a tale of lies. It's so bizarre.'

'Either she loves him so much that she'll put up with anything,' Ivy had said. 'Or she's a bloody fool. Actually, she's a fool anyway. I'd have left the moment I'd found out he was playing away.'

Whilst Holly drank the hot chocolate, Janet threw another log on the fire and left her to her thoughts. Mistletoe, who always seemed to know when Holly needed cheering up, came and curled up on her lap and Merlot, who was equally intuitive, was lying on Holly's boots, snoring rhythmically in time with the Christmas carols drifting from the pub radio.

One or two of the locals came in for a cup of coffee or 'the first drink of the day'. They asked Holly how she felt and told her what they thought of Gabriel. They wished that he'd remained lost and that Henry hadn't helped him find his way to Hideaway Down. Told her everything would turn out right, she'd see. And finally, they wished her well and left her in peace to dwell on her future prospects whilst they hovered around the bar and discussed who was likely to win this year's Best Mince Pie contest. As if there was any doubt.

The minutes ticked away, counted down by the number

of times Holly glanced at her watch, and the pendulum-like swaying of the red foil decorations.

At eleven-thirty, Ivy came bustling through the pub door, bringing with her an icy wind, a flurry of snow and news that Gabriel wasn't far behind her. She had finally tired of the ringing bell and the vibrating door and foolishly told him that "Holly isn't here. She's in The Snowdrop Inn and that was where she was going to stay".

'I'm sorry, Holly,' she said. 'But the man was driving me mad! I only beat him here because, despite the fact he has a Jaguar which could leave my car standing, I'm a faster driver.'

'He'd better not show that handsome, deceitful face of his in here,' Janet said, her hands on her hips. 'Frozen or not, he'll end up in the pond if he does.'

All faces turned to Janet as the door swung open for a second time in less than a minute. Gabriel Hardwick stood in the doorway of The Snowdrop Inn, snowflakes swirling around him like flies around dead meat, his face tight with a look of determination, his dark eyes scanning the pub.

Mistletoe woke up and hissed. Merlot leapt to her feet and barked. Holly skulked in her corner chair and hid behind her sister, camouflaged by a maze of pub regulars who'd come in within the last fifteen minutes.

'One more step and you'll end up in the pond,' Janet said. 'Ice or no ice.'

'I just want five minutes with Holly, Janet. That's all.'

'Don't you, "Janet" me. Only my friends can call me that. It's Mrs Gilroy to the likes of you. My daughter doesn't want to talk to you and neither do I, so go back where you came from and take that stuck-up girlfriend of yours with you.'

'Bryony is not my girlfriend, Jan... Mrs Gilroy.'

'Yeah. And I'm not Holly's mum – the woman who's

going to beat you to death if you don't get out of here.'

'She's not my girlfriend.'

'You shouldn't have treated Holly like that.'

'I said, Bryony's not my girlfriend. Why won't anyone listen to me?'

'Holly deserves better.'

'Of course she does. But Bryony's not my girlfriend.'

'Why didn't you just tell us the truth? Why did you lead my daughter on?'

'I did tell you the truth. I didn't lead Holly on.'

Henry Goode gave a loud cough, interrupting the tennis-like, back and forth debate.

'You told me you didn't have a girlfriend,' Henry said in a gruff voice, like a disappointed parent. 'Or a wife. Turns out you do have a girlfriend. Is a wife going to turn up next in our little village?

Gabriel laughed but the sound held no merriment. He shook his head.

'Henry, please. I don't have a girlfriend and I definitely don't have a wife. I can promise you that.'

'Then why did the woman say she was your girlfriend, eh! Answer me that.'

Gabriel shook his head once more. 'Because... she was my girlfriend. But now she's not.'

A chorus of gasps echoed around the pub.

'She says she is,' Janet jumped back in.

'Well, she's not. She was, for about two years. But I ended it.'

'Did you leave her a note?' Henry asked.

Gabriel frowned. 'No. I didn't leave her note. Why would I leave her note? Oh, I see. Well, I'm not like that. If I have something to say, I say it to a person's face. I told Bryony face-to-face that it was over. I explained how I felt and why I thought our relationship should end.'

131

'At Christmas? You ended a two-year relationship at Christmas? That's a bit harsh. Couldn't you have waited until after Christmas?'

'What, like New Year's Eve, you mean?'

Another chorus of gasps went out, louder this time.

'Wanker!' Ivy said, having remained oddly silent throughout the proceedings so far. 'It's beyond me why your girlfriend stays with you.'

'Oh for fuck's sake! She's not my bloody girlfriend!'

'Gabriel!' Henry boomed. 'There's no need to use language like that. Especially not to a young lady.'

Gabriel shook his head. 'I'm sorry, Ivy. I'm sorry, Henry. Everyone, I apologise. I'm sorry, Jan... Mrs Gilroy. It won't happen again. But for heaven's sake. Why won't any of you believe me? Bryony Dawes is *not* my girlfriend.'

'She says she's your agent too. Are you saying she lied about that as well?' Ivy questioned.

'No. No, that part's true. She is my agent.'

'I find that hard to believe,' Ivy said.

'Really? You're happy to believe she's my girlfriend – which she isn't, but you don't believe she's my agent – which she is.'

'I don't believe she'd still be your agent if it's true that you dumped her at Christmas. So if she's still your agent, she's obviously still your girlfriend.'

'I didn't dump her at Christmas. I dumped... I ended our relationship two months ago. Two. Months. Ago. Our personal relationship, that is. Not our business relationship. That relationship is still ongoing. Although after this little stunt she's pulled, I may soon be ending that one too.'

'At Christmas?' Henry gasped.

'Oh for...' Gabriel took a deep breath. 'May I please just talk to Holly?'

132

'No, Gabriel. You may not,' Janet said. 'And if you have any respect for us at all, you'll leave this pub right now.'

'It's for the best, Gabriel,' Henry said.

Gabriel looked around, let out a sigh as if he had the troubles of the world upon his shoulders, turned slowly on his heel and shoved the pub door open. It banged closed behind him, leaving a shower of snowflakes drifting silently to the floor, where they melted into a tiny puddle of water.

'Well!' Ned Stelling, who had been sitting by the bar when Ivy had burst in followed by Gabriel, suddenly and forcefully piped up: 'Either Gabriel's telling the truth, and that woman's lying, or vice versa. But I have to say this. I simply don't see what he's got to gain by coming here like that if she is his girlfriend. Surely it's better to upset us and leave here with his real relationship intact than to risk ruining a genuine relationship by rushing down here after Holly? And if Gabriel is lying, why did he say he'd broken up with the woman two months ago? Why not one, to make her non-acceptance more realistic? Or six, to make her seem like a stalker? Or simply say a few? Why two? It's so exact. Or am I missing the point entirely?'

Chapter Twenty-Four

Ned had a point. Holly had to give him that. And the more she thought about what both Ned and Gabriel had said, the more she believed that Gabriel was telling the truth. The only thing she didn't understand was why Bryony was still telling everyone that she was Gabriel's girlfriend. And wandering around the village wasn't making that any clearer to her. Until, outside The Coffee Hideaway, the café owned by her friend, Laurel French, she bumped slap bang into Paul.

'Holly!'

He looked like the cornered rat he was.

'Paul!'

She wasn't the love-sick girl she had been less than two days ago. Well, not love-sick for Paul Best, at any rate.

'What… what are you doing here?'

She'd heard mice squeak louder than that.

'Unlike you, Paul, I still live in Hideaway Down. Perhaps the question should be, what are you doing here?'

'I… I've come back to see my mum and dad. I didn't realise how much I would miss them by moving to Australia.'

'But surely, with Skype and all the other video-chatting apps and services available, you can see them every day and it's just like being with them, isn't it? At least, that's what you told me every time I said I'd miss my mum and Ivy.'

Paul gave a little cough and looked flustered.

'Okay, so you were right and I was wrong. I'm sorry,

Holly. I'm truly sorry.'

'For the video-chat argument? Or for dumping me for my best friend after fifteen years together? Or for the delightfully brief note you and Naomi slipped through the door of Holly Cottage? Or for leaving me standing in the centre of The Snowdrop Inn five minutes before the stroke of midnight last New Year's Eve, wondering where you were?'

Paul flinched and closed his eyes as if trying to shut out the memory of it all.

'For all of it,' he said. 'But most of all, for failing to realise what I had. For thinking there was someone better. For dumping you. I thought you were holding me back. I thought Hideaway Down was a dead-end place to live. I thought Australia would give me a fresh start. I was completely wrong on all counts.'

Holly knew she was blinking. She knew her mouth had fallen open; she could feel the cold air stabbing at the back of her throat. What she didn't know was whether she could believe her ears. Was Paul saying what she thought he was?

'You look good, Holly. So, so good. It cuts me up just looking at you.'

'Where's Naomi?' Holly managed.

'What? Oh. I don't know. Well, I know where she's going. I just don't know where she is at the moment.'

'Going?'

He nodded. 'To her parents' house. In Eastbourne. I've been a complete fool, Holly. A total and utter idiot. Can you ever forgive me? Will you forgive me?'

Holly took a tiny step backwards. 'I… I do forgive you, Paul. But I'm not quite sure what you're saying. Have you and Naomi had a row?'

Paul nodded frenetically. 'More than a row, Holly. A monumental bust up. I've finally seen the light.'

'You... you've broken up with Naomi? At Christmas?'
This was unbelievable. Truly unbelievable.
'What does it matter when? What matters is, it's over.'
'What on earth did you row about? You arrived together yesterday. I heard someone in the pub mention they'd seen you together. Was the row last night? Or this morning? When did she leave?'
'It started last night and carried on this morning. She left after breakfast. And the row was about you.'
'Me? Why did you row about me?'
'Because when someone phoned Mum last night and told her how badly your new boyfriend had treated you, I went ballistic. But I was also glad the guy had lied. I suddenly realised I still loved you. And Naomi realised it too.

Holly burst out laughing. She hadn't meant to but this was just too ridiculous.
'Are you... are you, by the remotest possibility, telling me that you want me back?'
Paul stepped forward and took her in his arms. He had obviously assumed her laughter was that of joy, not pure amusement.
'That's exactly what I'm telling you. I didn't think Hideaway Down had anything to offer me. But it does, Holly. It has you. I'm coming back, Holly. We can start again.'
He moved in for a kiss but she pushed him away.
'Oh no we can't. And if the only thing you think Hideaway Down has to offer you, is me, you're sadly mistaken. It does not. This may surprise you, Paul. It's certainly surprised me. But I don't love you any longer. And I don't want you back. I'm sorry, but there it is. And as it's Christmas, I'll give you the gift of my advice. Go after Naomi and beg her to take you back. Goodbye, Paul.

And Merry Christmas.'

Holly pushed open the door of The Coffee Hideaway and *God Rest Ye Merry Gentlemen* greeted her.

'Hello Laurel,' she said, with a beaming smile. 'May I have a mug of hot chocolate, please, with whipped cream and all the trimmings?

'Hello Holly.' Laurel smiled back. 'Coming right up. What was all that about with Paul? I saw him put his arms around you. Don't tell me the guy has finally come to his senses and wants you back.'

Holly shook her head. 'No. We were just saying goodbye to the past and letting bygones be bygones. It is Christmas, after all.'

The delicious aromas of chocolate and coffee wafted around the cosy café as she waited for her hot chocolate. The snow was coming down harder now and she watched the Christmas shoppers dashing to and fro along Market Street, whilst she sang along to the Christmas carols on the radio.

Chapter Twenty-Five

The Best Mince Pie contest always attracted a crowd but this year's crowd struggled to fit inside the church hall. Every inch of the wooden building was jam-packed, like Christmas crackers in a box.

Holly, Ivy, Janet and Gramps were sitting in the front row, holding hands and waiting nervously for the judges' decision. Holly had never entered the contest before, in spite of Ivy telling her every year that she should but as she'd sat in The Coffee Hideaway mulling over the past few days, she had made a decision. It was time for a change.

From now on, instead of sitting around waiting for things to happen, she would chase life down, grab it by its tail and show it she wasn't scared of anything. She would live life to the full, no matter what. She would take risks; ask for what she wanted and pursue her dreams, wherever they may lead.

She may not win The Best Mince Pie contest; in fact, she knew she wouldn't, but winning wasn't everything. What was important was taking part.

Maisy Miller, Sarah Saltcote and Bartram Battersfold inched their way along the line of trellis tables, each of which was covered with a festive tablecloth. The three judges dutifully munched their way through eight separate mince pies, sampling a mince pie from the plate of every one of the eight contestants. The plates were all identical and the contestants' identities were kept secret until the judges reached their final decision and the winner was revealed.

The winner would be chosen based purely on the quality of the product. This included the texture of the pastry, the sweetness of the contents, the quantity of the filling and the variety of flavours dancing on the tongue on that first bite. The pastry case needed to hold its precious load securely without bits of the syrupy texture oozing out and making fingers sticky. The filling also had to be just right, not too syrupy or too dry. So many small things to be taken into account but when each one was marked up, the mince pie with the highest score was proclaimed The Best Mince Pie in Hideaway Down.

Finally, after half an hour of tense anticipation, head judge, Bartram Battersfold stood behind the plate on which the winning mince pies sat. He slid the plate over a few inches to reveal the card beneath on which the winner's name was written.

'The winner is...' He smiled and glanced down at the card. 'Pet... Oh good heavens! This can't be. There must be a mistake. I mean... That is. Um. I didn't realise you had entered the contest, Holly. What a lovely surprise.'

Bartram didn't look happy.

'Are you saying Holly's won then, Bartram?' Ivy yelled at the top of her lungs. 'Only you didn't make that clear. Is my sister the winner of this year's The Best Mince Pie contest?'

'What? Oh dear me. Yes. Yes, she is. The winner of The Best Mince Pie contest is: Miss Holly Gilroy. Congratulations, Holly. Do come up and get your prize.'

No one was more surprised than Holly except perhaps Bartram Battersfold. She stood up to cheers and hoots and shouts of 'Congratulations, Holly!'

Petunia Welsley rushed up to her, smelling heavenly as always, and gave Holly a genuinely congratulatory hug.

'Well done, Holly. I'm so pleased for you. I've eaten

your mince pies at The Snowdrop Bash over the years and I know how delicious they are. Congratulations!'

'That's our girl,' Janet shouted.

'Thank you!' Holly said, wiping a solitary tear of joy from her cheek. 'I don't know what to say.'

Bartram handed her the wooden rolling pin which had the words, 'You're The Best Mince Pie Maker in Hideaway Down' etched into one side of it. He shook her hand and repeated his congratulations.

Holly looked around the room at all the cheering faces and sparkling eyes and her heart swelled with a sense of achievement... until her eyes met Gabriel's. He was standing just inside the door, staring at her, a congratulatory smile spread wide across his sensual lips, his hands clapping louder than anyone else's. Or perhaps she was imagining that. He was definitely clapping wildly though. Their eyes held for several seconds until Ivy rushed up and broke the spell by sweeping her off her feet in a bone-crushing hug.

'I told you, you could do it! I don't know who was more surprised. You or old Bartram.' Ivy was clearly overjoyed.

Holly looked back for Gabriel but he had disappeared.

'Yes. And at least it proves that the contest isn't rigged.'

Ivy cleared her throat and dragged Holly away from the crowds, who were now drinking tea and sampling the extra mince pies all the contestants brought with them for that very purpose.

'Actually, it proves it was.'

'What? Oh no. Ivy, please don't tell me you cheated somehow to let me win.'

She shook her head. 'On the contrary, I cheated to stop you losing.'

'What?'

'As you know, Ned's mum is the person who sets out

the plates each year. I was talking to her yesterday in the pub and I asked her how she decides which contestants' mince pies to put where or whether she simply lay them out in a random fashion – which you would sort of hope she would, wouldn't you? Anyway, as wonderful as Audrey Stelling is, she's not too bright and she told me that Bartram insists the contestants' names go in alphabetical order, from left to right, a to z.'

'You're kidding? That's cheating. He knows the names of all the contestants, so he knows which mince pies belong to whom. Oh wait. He didn't know I was entering. I handed mine into Audrey only five minutes before the start.'

'Duh. You're being as daft as Audrey is. It doesn't matter who enters because unless there's a contestant whose surname begins with a W, X, Y or Z, Petunia's mince pies will always be at the very end. And if a Miss Xenophobe does enter, Petunia's mince pies would be second to the end. Until today, that is.'

'Oh yes, I see. Ivy, what did you do?'

'I merely told Audrey that I didn't really think that was fair and when I explained it, she agreed. So she said that regardless of what Bartram had said, she would put the plates out randomly. If Petunia's mince pies were better than yours, she would've won fairly and squarely. She didn't, you did. And I don't think Bartram will cheat next year, now that he knows he's been rumbled.

Holly burst out laughing. This day had turned out much better than she had expected. And how good it had been to see Gabriel clapping for her so enthusiastically. If only she could share her joy with him. But never mind that. She could share it with her family and friends and that was more than enough for her.

Chapter Twenty-Six

By the time Holly finally left the hall, it was five-thirty and snowing heavily. Market Street was covered in a blanket of white, and a kaleidoscope of colours cavorted over it from the reflections of the street lamps, the brightly-lit shop windows and the multi-coloured Christmas lights. Holly wrapped her coat more tightly around her, buried her head deep in her collar and walked towards The Snowdrop Inn.

Her mum had left soon after congratulating her, together with Ivy and Gramps. Having closed the pub for three quarters of an hour so that they could all support her in the contest, they needed to get back and reopen.

Holly had been dreading Christmas this year but as she passed one shop window after another, she admired their festive displays and their promises of cheer. She would enjoy this Christmas come what may. It would have been nice to enjoy it with Gabriel but some things just weren't meant to be – like the shop she stopped outside of now, its windows bare save for a 'To Let' sign. A young, hip couple had moved down from London and rented it for six months but sex toys and the like weren't quite the thing for Hideaway Down or its visitors it seemed, and the couple moved to Brighton when the tenancy expired.

It was such a shame. Not because she particularly wanted a sex shop close at hand – if she wanted stuff like that, she would get it on the internet – but because it was a pretty little shop with wooden shelves on every wall and double doors between two, square bay windows. It had been a travel agents for many years, independently owned and run, but when the owners retired it was taken over by a large charity organisation for a time. The powers that be decided it wasn't economically viable so its doors were closed and had remained closed for several months until the young couple had taken it on. It was sad to see it empty once again. Surely someone would see its potential?

Holly walked on. The snow was really coming down and the sooner she got back to the welcoming warmth of The Snowdrop Inn, the better. She would curl up in front of one of the fires for twenty minutes, with a mug of her mum's delicious hot chocolate and the Gabriella Mann romance she still hadn't had a chance to finish. There was nothing quite as nice as curling up with a good book and stepping into a world lovingly created by any of her favourite authors.

She stopped in her tracks. Her mind whirred like the wheels of the steam train on the nearby vintage railway line, slowly gathering speed.

Was it possible? Could she do it? Could she afford to try? She smiled. She could at least make a few enquiries. What did she have to lose? She could write a business plan and if it worked on paper, why not give it a go? Hadn't she decided it was time she took life by the tail?

She backtracked to the forest green frontage of the shop and stared through the window, picturing how it might look. With every passing second her excitement grew, along with a healthy dose of rationality. She must be sensible and not let her heart rule her head, but even so…

'Congratulations!'

The voice made her jump. Gabriel's voice. She recognised it instantly. She took a deep breath and turned to face him.

'Thank you.'

They stared silently at one another for several seconds.

'I wish I'd tried one of your mince pies now. I'm obviously missing something rather special.'

'It's not too late. You can have some tomorrow for afternoon tea. I'll tell Ivy.'

'Ivy?'

'Yes. She's… she's looking after the cottages for a couple of days and I'm working in the pub. We've switched jobs.'

'Because of me?'

'No. Because of me. Where's your girl… where's Bryony? Has she settled in? Will you be staying for the holidays as planned?'

He took a step closer.

She took a step back.

'Holly. I know what everyone is saying. I know what everyone thinks. But I swear to you it isn't true. Bryony is not my girlfriend. She was for two years but I ended the relationship two months ago. Please believe me, I'm not lying. What would be the point?'

She studied his face. He *was* telling the truth. She could see it in his eyes. But still…

'I do believe you, Gabriel. For some reason, it seems that Bryony doesn't. Ivy told me that Bryony was still at the cottage today. That means she spent the night. Ivy cottage only has one bedroom.'

His eyes opened wide. 'Yes. And Bryony slept in it. I slept on the sofa. Although I didn't get much sleep.'

'But she's staying?'

'Not if I can do anything about it.'

'And can you? Do something about it?'

He licked his bottom lip. 'I hope so, Holly. But it's… It's complicated.'

'Because she's your agent, you mean?'

'Partly because of that.'

144

'What's the other part?'

He frowned and ran a gloved hand through his hair.

'As I said, it's complicated.'

'Well then, I think you need to deal with that, without adding even further... complications. I should get back. They'll be wondering where I've got to.'

She turned to walk away but he grabbed her arm.

'Holly. If I do deal with that. If I can sort out... the complications. Will you...? Would you...?'

'*If* you can? You're not sure? Just how... complicated is it? Oh my God. She's not... pregnant, is she?'

She pulled her arm away and took another step back.

'No! No definitely not.'

'Then what?'

He didn't answer. He just stared into her eyes.

She tried again. 'Is it something to do with your business relationship?' A sudden laugh escaped her. 'Is there something in your contract saying you must go out with her or else?'

Something flickered across his eyes and he looked away.

'That's not as far from the truth as you might imagine.'

'Oh come on, Gabriel. I was joking. I'm not an idiot. Agents can't tell authors who to date.'

'Bryony can. Or thinks she can. I want to tell you, Holly. I really do. But this is serious. It's complicated, as I said. I need to sort it out. I need to deal with Bryony.'

'Then deal with Bryony. Don't stand here talking about it.'

'Please don't hate me, Holly.'

'I don't hate you. Far from it. I wish you'd tell me what the problem is but I understand if you feel you can't. You know where I am if you change your mind.'

He brightened at that.

'You'll talk to me?'

'I'm talking to you now, aren't I?'

He smiled and nodded.

'I wasn't sure if you would. I hoped you would. That's why I waited for you to come out. I didn't want everyone watching us.'

'You waited? After I saw you at the contest, you waited for me to leave?'

'Yes. In there.'

He nodded his head towards The Coffee Hideaway and Holly laughed again.

'Did Laurel give you a hard time? She's a good friend of mine, and feels very protective of me.'

'Everyone in the village seems very protective of you, and yes, she did a bit. But that's okay. I've dealt with worse. And I knew she had your interests at heart. And speaking of hearts, I don't suppose I should be saying this but I overheard a conversation while I was in the café. A conversation about you and Paul. That's why I didn't come out the moment I saw you. I'm half ashamed to say this, but I wanted to hear what they said.'

'Oh? And what did they say?'

'That you've forgiven him. That you've let go of the past. But someone else said he'd asked you to go out with him again – to try once more. They said they'd heard that he dumped Naomi in the hope of getting back with you. Is that true?'

Holly shrugged. 'Let's just say, he's been missing Hideaway Down. It's true that I've forgiven him.'

'So... There's a chance you might get back together?'

'No, Gabriel. There's absolutely no chance of that. I'm looking to the future, not the past.'

She glanced at the empty shop and smiled. Gabriel stood silently by her side, snow dancing around their shoulders.

'This would make a perfect bookshop,' he said, after a

while.

Her eyes shot to his profile. Could he read her mind?

'That is precisely what I've been thinking.'

He turned his head and met her eyes, a large smile appearing on his lips.

'It seems we're both making plans for our futures. I'd love to hear what you have in mind and if I can help in any way, you only have to ask.'

'Ditto,' she said. 'But deal with Bryony first.'

'I'll deal with her today. She'll be gone by tomorrow. But first, I'll walk you to the pub.'

Chapter Twenty-Seven

Tuesday, 22nd December

'Have you heard the news?'

Meg Stanbridge, her cherubic face the colour of cranberry sauce, burst into The Snowdrop Inn and waddled towards the bar, followed closely by Ivy.

'What news?' Janet asked, glancing in Holly's direction.

Holly continued pulling Henry's pint, but met her mother's look. Last night, Holly had told her family about her conversation with Gabriel and the fact that she believed him.

She'd also told them of her intention of looking into the possibility of opening a bookshop – which they all supported wholeheartedly. So much so in fact that she and her mum had sat up until the small hours, working on a business plan. By the time they'd finished, it was three a.m. and Holly had spent the night in her old room at the pub, rather than drive back to Holly Cottage in the snow.

Meg placed one chubby hand on her chest and took several deep breaths as Janet and Holly looked across at Ivy.

'I know nothing,' Ivy said, with a shrug.

'Lordy, Lordy me. Where to start?' Meg said. 'Pour me a rum and black please, Ivy, there's a dear and let me catch my breath.'

'I'm not working here today. I... oh never mind.'

Ivy went behind the bar and poured Meg her drink. Meg knocked it back in one and held the glass out for a refill.

'It's so cold out there. I need to warm these old bones. My poor darling geese don't know what to do with themselves. They've been in and out the woodshed all morning. Can hardly see them amongst so much snow. If it wasn't for their orange bills and bright blue eyes, I swear you'd think they were a snowdrift.'

'And it's still coming down,' Janet said. 'I believe you said you had some news, Meg. Was that it? About the Gaggle Gang?'

'Lordy, Lordy, no. It's about dear Petunia and that old fool, Bartram.'

Holly let out the breath she had been holding, met her mum's eyes, and shrugged. Ivy passed Meg another rum and black. Meg took a sip and climbed onto a stool.

'After our dear Holly won The Best Mince Pie contest, old Bartram didn't know what to do with himself. Proper flustered, he was. Thought he'd have a heart attack, I did. Spent a good twenty minutes apologising and commiserating with dear Petunia. Not that Petunia was in the least bit put out not to have won. Said your mince pies were delicious, she did. But old Bartram, like the fool that man is, wouldn't let it be. Doesn't know how it happened, he says. Bleating and blurting stuff out all over the place, he was. Finally, he tells her the whole thing's been rigged for all these years. Can you believe it?'

'I always knew it was,' Janet said. 'Nothing against Petunia's mince pies, of course. They're definitely delicious but I always said there was something not quite right about that contest.'

'What did Petunia say when she found out?' Ivy asked, leaning her elbows on the bar.

'I don't suppose she was happy,' Holly said.

'Well, there's the funny thing.' Meg took another sip of her drink and shook her head of grey, dishevelled curls.

'She asks him why he did it, and the old fool blurts out that he loves her, he does.'

'Good heavens!' Janet laughed. 'Just like that?'

Meg's curls bounced as she nodded.

'How did Petunia take that?' Holly asked.

'I bet she's still running,' Ivy said. 'She's probably reached Portsmouth by now.'

Holly grinned. 'Not in this weather.'

'Well, that's the best bit,' Meg continued. 'Old Bartram's blubbering and spluttering and saying he expects she'll never want to speak to him again, and what does Petunia do?'

'Punch him on that snub nose of his?' Ivy suggested.

'Lordy, Lordy, no. Worse than that. Grabs his face in her hands, she does. And kisses him. Smack bang on the lips. Kisses him! Can you believe it?'

'She... what?!' Ivy looked incredulous. 'Was she drunk? Because she'd have to be to want to kiss Bartram.'

Meg shook her head and cackled.

'Must've been very drunk then. Spent the night with him, she did. Our dear Maisy saw it with her very own eyes, she did. She'd just put another batch of buns in her oven and was setting out the first lot in the bakery window, she was. Saw Petunia leave Bartram's at just gone six this morning, she did. And we all know Bartram doesn't open till eight on the dot, so Petunia wasn't in there buying sausages, she wasn't. Lordy, Lordy me, no.'

'Ew! I feel sick,' Ivy said. 'Petunia and Bartram.' She shook visibly. 'It doesn't bear thinking about. I need a drink. That's left a nasty taste in my mouth.'

'Don't be mean, darling,' Janet said. 'It takes all sorts to make a world. Bartram's not that bad and in his younger days, he was quite good looking. I'm happy for him. I'm happy for them both. And you see, girls, it just goes to show I'm right. There's a man out there for every one of us.'

'If mine looks anything like Bartram, I'm joining a convent,' Ivy said, shaking every part of her body for maximum effect.

'I would have been here earlier, I would,' Meg said, emptying her glass. 'But I had to chat to my geese and make sure they were comfy, I did. So I didn't get out till late. Only just heard, I have. Pour me another, Ivy dear.' She smoothed her hair back in place and smiled contentedly. Suddenly, she straightened her back and her eyes opened wide. 'Lordy, Lordy me. Almost forgot, I did. Not the only news I have. But you've probably already heard it, being as it's about you, dear Holly in a manner of speaking, it is.'

Holly, Ivy and Janet exchanged glances and waited.

And waited.

And waited.

'Well?' Ivy said. 'What news?' She handed Meg her third drink.

'Lordy, Lordy me. I thought you knew, I did.'

'We don't,' Holly said.

'Oh my.'

'Perhaps you'd be kind enough to tell us, Meg?' Janet coaxed.

'They've had a row.'

'Who has?' Janet asked, throwing Holly an encouraging look.

'That woman who came in here dressed up like a dog's dinner, and that author who got lost. Harry heard it, he did when he was delivering the milk. Screaming like a banshee she was. Didn't like the look of her, I didn't. Moment I saw her I thought there's a proper madam, I did. Nasty piece of work.' She shook her head and took two large gulps of her drink.

Holly straightened out a bar cloth and studied her fingers. 'What else did Harry say?'

'Nothing I can think of. Left them to it, he did.' She gulped down the remainder of her drink and clambered off the stool. 'Lordy, Lordy me. Can't sit around here chatting all day, I can't. Bingo in the church hall to get to. You all take care. See you soon, I will.'

'Does she ever pay for her drinks?' Ivy asked, as Meg waddled towards the door.

'Not in my lifetime,' Janet replied. 'But she gives us eggs and fresh veg. from her crop whenever she can so it all works out in the end. Besides, even if she didn't, today's news was worth three rum and blacks.'

Holly turned to Ivy. 'You didn't call to say you'd heard a row this morning.'

Ivy blushed and looked away. 'I didn't hear it. I must've been in the shower or something.'

Holly watched her for several seconds. 'Yes. That must have been the reason. The only question is, whose shower were you in? I get the feeling it wasn't the one at Holly Cottage.'

Chapter Twenty-Eight

Gabriel walked into The Snowdrop Inn and a sea of faces turned in his direction. The cacophony of voices fell silent until the only sounds were the cheery Christmas carols playing on the radio, and Merlot, barking.

Gabriel searched for Holly's face amongst the crowd and he spotted her behind the bar.

'She's leaving,' he said. 'Bryony is leaving.'

'Your girlfriend?' Someone at the back of the pub queried.

'She is not my girlfriend.'

'Please let's not start that again,' Ivy pleaded. 'I almost lost the will to live the last time.'

'In this weather?' Henry asked. 'Nasty on the roads out there.'

'I'm sure she'll be careful but she's used to driving in the snow. She has a chalet in the French Alps and goes there several times during the ski season.'

'Ooh, lah-di-dah,' one of the customers piped up.

'They clear the roads in the Alps,' Janet remarked. 'Our local council's not quite so diligent. We'll be lucky if we see a snowplough this side of New Year.'

'Nevertheless, I'm sure she'll be fine. May I come in for a drink please, Mrs Gilroy?'

Janet glanced at Holly, who nodded.

'You may,' Janet said. 'And you can call me Janet. But I'm telling you now, Gabriel Hardwick, if any more girlfriends or wives show up, you'll be in that pond faster than any of the Gaggle Gang can shake their tail feathers.

153

You hear me?'

'I hear you... Janet. Loud and clear. I promise you, no more girlfriends and definitely no wives.'

'Then what would you like to drink?'

'A pint of beer, please. I don't mind which. I just need a drink. This hasn't been one of my better mornings, although it is starting to look brighter by the minute.'

He smiled at Holly and made his way towards her.

'Brighter by the minute?' another customer chipped in as Gabriel walked past. 'Looks as dark as the devil out there. No sign of this snow easing so far as I can see.'

'He's an author,' another said. 'Vivid imagination.'

'No sense of direction,' said another. 'He's the author who got lost.'

'Leave him be,' someone else said. 'Holly likes him. That's good enough for us.'

Gabriel's smile widened. Hideaway Down may not be Shangri-La but it seemed like paradise to him.

'So what happened?' Ivy asked, before he'd even reached the bar.

'Ivy!' Holly said. 'Give the man a chance. You said, "leaving", Gabriel. Does that mean she's still at Ivy Cottage at the moment?'

'Yes. She wasn't very happy. I thought I should give her a bit of space. I said I was coming to the pub and she promised she'd be gone by the time I got back this afternoon.'

'I hope she doesn't wreck the place,' Ivy said. 'You hear of women who do that for revenge. For my part, if she wants to trash your place, that's fine with me, but most of the stuff in Ivy Cottage doesn't belong to you. You only brought your laptop, some clothes and a few other bits and pieces. I hope she doesn't rip the sofa to shreds with a pair of scissors.'

154

'Bryony may be a little... volatile at times but I don't think she would do that. I don't think she's that kind of woman. But then... No. No, I'm sure she wouldn't do anything like that.'

'Hmm,' Ivy continued. 'You don't sound too sure about that. I know the place is insured but does insurance cover the acts of women scorned? Or is that one of the exclusions, a bit like war and acts of God?'

'Perhaps I shouldn't leave her alone up there? Perhaps I should go back and make sure everything is okay?'

Holly frowned at Ivy and smiled at Gabriel. 'I'm sure there's nothing to worry about. Ivy's just winding you up. Ignore her. Unless of course you think there is the slightest chance that Bryony might do something.'

Would she? Would she really be that unpleasant? Was she that kind of woman? The truth is, he didn't really know the answer. Perhaps he'd better go and check. Better to be safe than sorry.

He took several gulps of his beer and put the half empty glass on the bar.

'I don't really think she would, but there's no harm in being on the safe side. I'll go back to the cottage and I'll come back here when she's gone. I'll see you later, Holly.'

'You hope,' Ivy said, with a wicked grin. 'It might not just be the sofa she takes the scissors to.'

Gabriel sneered. 'Yes. Thanks so much for pointing that out, Ivy.'

Ivy's grin widened. 'Anything to help. You know me.'

Gabriel shook his head and smiled at Holly. 'I'll be back.'

He'd only taken two steps towards the door when it suddenly burst open with a bitter cold blast of air and a cloud of snow. Bryony was standing in the doorway.

'Bryony! What are you doing here? I thought we'd said

155

everything there is to say.'

Once again the entire pub fell silent and this time Janet even switched off the radio. Merlot didn't bark though; she growled.

'You may have, Gabriel. But I haven't. Besides, I wanted to come and see for myself what's so special about this woman for whom you are apparently prepared to sacrifice everything. Especially if it's true that you only met her on Friday. Although frankly, darling, you know I don't believe that for a second. Which one is the little tramp?'

'Sacrifice everything for?' Holly queried.

'Does she think you and Gabriel already knew one another?' Ivy asked.

And Janet immediately said, 'Did you just call my daughter a tramp? You jumped-up tart. Let me through. I'll make sure that Botoxed face of yours matches your inflated, blood-red lips.'

Janet pushed her way out from behind the bar but Gabriel caught her arm, shook his head and held her back.

'I'll deal with this, Janet. I apologise on her behalf.'

He glanced at Ned, who instantly eased Janet back towards the bar. With an apologetic smile at Holly, Gabriel turned back to face Bryony.

'I think you should leave, Bryony. Right now. Or I shall have to make you.'

'Now who's bandying threats?'

'It's not a threat. It's a fact. Do us both a favour. Leave right now.'

Clearly undaunted, Bryony continued: 'Is this where you came on your so-called "research trips", Gabriel? To have it off in some dreadful little hovel with a virginal, country bumpkin who's just like one of those mealy-mouthed heroines in your novels.'

Gabriel marched towards her.

'That is offensive on so many levels, I won't even bother answering. And let's not forget, Bryony, those "mealy-mouthed heroines" as you've suddenly decided to call them, have made each of us a small fortune.'

'And they could make us multimillionaires if you'll just see sense and do as I ask.'

'As you demand, don't you mean? Are you leaving? Or do I need to... assist you?'

'Gabriel! Darling! You're throwing away the chance of a lifetime. When Hollywood calls with an offer like this, you don't suddenly develop scruples and turn it down. You grab it with both hands and enjoy it.'

'Out!' Gabriel said. 'Not another word, Bryony. I mean it.'

'You're being ridiculous. It's what your grandmother always dreamed of.'

He grabbed her arm and forcefully dragged her through the doorway.

'You haven't the slightest idea what my grandmother dreamed of. And even if you had, you wouldn't care unless you thought you could make money out of it. And that, Bryony, is your problem. I think it's best if we call it a day professionally in addition to personally. I'll contact my lawyers today.'

'Gabriel! Gabriel, stop!'

He dragged her out of the pub to her car and forced her inside.

'Leave right now, Bryony, or I swear to God I'll call the tabloids myself and tell them everything.'

She hesitated for a moment, looked up at his face and switched on her ignition. The engine roared into life and, with a shower of snow, she sped off into the twilight.

Gabriel turned around and blinked. Every single person

157

who had been inside The Snowdrop Inn was outside, on the bank, but was now hurrying back inside, as if they hoped he hadn't seen them.

He would have laughed if he hadn't been so furious. Not just with Bryony, but also with himself.

Chapter Twenty-Nine

'What was that all about?' Ivy asked Holly and Janet as they scampered back behind the bar.

'I have no idea,' Holly replied.

And she hadn't. Gabriel had told her that things were complicated but what had Bryony meant when she'd said that Gabriel was sacrificing everything for a woman he'd just met? Was Bryony referring to her? And research trips? And scruples? And Hollywood? And why had Gabriel been so cross when Bryony had mentioned his grandmother?

Then there was the bit about the tabloids. Why would Gabriel say he'd call the tabloids himself? And from the way he had phrased it, it sounded as if it was something that Bryony had previously threatened. Why would the tabloids be interested in Gabriel? Unless there was something he was keeping hidden – some deep, dark secret.

There was no point in speculating. He'd either explain it or he wouldn't. She'd have to wait and see. But one thing was for certain. Whether Gabriel wanted it to or not, nothing would happen between them until he'd told her everything.

Gabriel stomped back into the pub with a face like thunder and eyes like bolt lightning.

'I'm very sorry you all had to witness that,' he said, striding towards Holly.

'It wasn't your fault,' said Janet. 'Although I don't think much of your past taste in women.'

'Nor do I,' he said, with a wan smile. 'I assure you, it's improved.' He met Holly's eyes. 'I need to talk to you please, Holly. There are some things I need to tell you. If you still want to hear them after that display, that is. I hope you do. I can explain.'

'I want to hear them,' Ivy said. 'So if Holly doesn't want to listen, you can tell me and I'll tell her. Of course, I'll probably tell the entire village too, but...' She smiled and shrugged.

Holly tutted and shook her head. 'Thanks, Ivy. But I'd rather hear it from Gabriel. Now? Do you want to talk now?'

He looked flustered and unsure.

'I do but...' He leaned in closer and lowered his voice. 'I think I need to call my lawyer first. I know that sounds bizarrely dramatic but there are legal implications regarding part of what I want to tell you, and Bryony wasn't very happy as you could no doubt tell. I need to check whether there's anything I must do before I tell you.'

'Have you... Is it something illegal?'

'No. But there're certain clauses in my contracts with both Bryony and my publishers and I'd rather not give anyone the slightest cause to sue me or, more importantly, drag my grandmother's name through the mud. Don't worry, Holly, it's nothing serious. It's just something that's important to me. Would you give me a couple of hours please, to make some calls? My laptop's at the cottage so I need to go back there.'

Holly nodded. 'Yes. I could meet you at the cottage later if you like.'

'Perfect. Why don't we...? I mean... I'd like to cook supper for you, as we planned on Sunday night. Would you join me for supper? Just supper. And to talk. Nothing else, I promise.'

'Yes. I'll have to clear it with Mum and Ivy because I should be working here this evening, but I'm sure it'll be fine. Especially as they're eavesdropping.'

She turned her head towards them and they pretended they weren't listening. Ivy poured Ned a pint and Janet grabbed a cloth and wiped down the bar.

Gabriel smiled. 'Let's say seven then. I'll see you later, Holly. Bye Ivy, bye Janet. Give my regards to Gramps.' He turned to face the crowded room and raised his voice by an octave or two. 'Bye everyone. See you tomorrow.'

'Bye Gabriel,' came the unified reply.

Holly laughed. It was obvious that the entire ensemble had been straining their ears to hear as much as they possibly could.

Chapter Thirty

Gabriel took Holly's coat and hung it up. She may have only come from next door, but it was freezing outside and since it had stopped snowing, the temperature seemed to have plummeted further.

'Go into the sitting room,' he said. 'I've lit the wood burner and poured you a glass of wine. I'll join you in a second. I just need to check on supper.'

Holly smiled. 'Whatever it is, it smells delicious.'

Gabriel smiled back. 'It's lasagne. I'm afraid my cooking skills are limited. They seem to involve mince and pasta, or pasta and mince.'

'Two of my favourite dishes.'

'And mine. But that could be because they're the only things I can cook. I'll be with you in a moment.'

He dashed into the kitchen, checked everything was fine, took several deep breaths and returned to join Holly.

She was looking round the room, her eyes alight with pleasure and surprise. Suddenly, he saw a cloud of doubt pass over them.

'When did you put these up?'

She was referring to the Christmas decorations and it was obvious that she was wondering whose handiwork the display was. His, or possibly Bryony's.

'I fixed the tree in the stand on Sunday night but that was all I did. For obvious reasons. I didn't feel very festive yesterday so I did all this, this afternoon, after I'd spoken to my lawyers and made a few other calls. Does it look okay? Is it festive enough? Are there enough lights?'

Holly's laugh rang out like tiny, jingling bells.

'It's beautiful. The tree looks stunning in that corner and all those vintage style decorations suit this cottage perfectly. The lights are wonderful. And the way you've wound some around the room brings colour to every nook and cranny and brightens every shadow. I'm impressed. You clearly didn't need any supervision.'

'All I need to do now is to buy some presents to go under the tree. I met the kids next door this afternoon. I'd already met Robin. Today, he introduced me to his wife, Tabby and their kids, Lulu and Sean. The family's had a pretty rough year by the sounds of it, although none of them grumbled or whined. Tabby's had serious health problems but she's doing well now and expected to recover fully. They didn't go into details but I get the impression it was cancer or something similar. So I thought I'd get some presents for the kids.'

'That's a lovely idea.'

'I'll give them to Robin and Tabby on Christmas Eve before I head down to The Snowdrop Bash. That's if I'm still welcome, of course. I know you and Ivy won't be here as you'll be helping your mum and Gramps so I'll see you at the party. Assuming you're talking to me after tonight. Will I see you on Christmas Day?'

She smiled encouragingly. 'I suppose that depends on what you tell me.'

Gabriel took a deep breath. 'I'd better get on with it then, but I'm not sure where to start.'

'Dare I say, at the beginning?'

'Right. I think I told you that it was because of my gran that I became an author.'

Holly nodded. 'Yes, you did.'

Gabriel cleared his throat. 'What I didn't tell you, I don't think, is that Gran was an author too. As she got older, her eyesight deteriorated. She found it difficult to read or write for prolonged periods and looking at a computer screen became virtually impossible. I'd just come back from a year of travelling and I was doing some freelance work to pay the bills. This was ten years ago when I was twenty-five. Gran asked me to help her and even though I'd have done it for free, she insisted on paying me. She would dictate to me and I would type out her manuscript. A bit like a secretary really. Then one day, I made a brief comment on a particular chapter and she liked my suggestion. After that, she started asking my opinion on everything she wrote and from there it sort of progressed into me writing the books and Gran commenting on them.'

He topped up Holly's wine glass and tossed another log in the wood burner.

'So effectively, your ghostwriting career began with your gran?'

'And ended with my gran's death. I only wrote for her. No one else. When her book deal ended, she was offered a new one. She told her agent and her publisher that to all intents and purposes, I was the one now writing all her books and she would merely give me feedback on how to improve a particular scene or chapter. She said that I should be the one offered the contract – although I didn't know that at the time. They were reluctant on two counts. One, because I was an unknown author other than the fact that I was her grandson, and two, because I am male.'

'Male? I understand the unknown author part. Publishers are often reluctant to take on someone whose commercial viability can't be guaranteed but I don't understand the problem with your gender. Men have a far better chance than women of being published, apart from in certain genres like romance, for example. Did... did your grandmother write romance?'

'She did.'

'So… You've been writing romance novels? For several years?'

'I have.'

He could see how surprised Holly was from the look in her eyes then a furrow appeared between her brows.

'What happened then?'

'They offered me a contract but on the basis that I wrote under Gran's name. Gran wanted at the very least to say the books were co-authored but she'd built up her name after many years and had – still has – a substantial fan base. It was felt that adding a man's name would possibly have a detrimental effect on sales. Gran wanted to stand her ground but I believed it was more important to keep her name alive and her fans happy. Fame doesn't interest me. It never has. And I was being paid very well so I was happy to continue. Her agent, Bryony, persuaded her, with my help, that keeping the status quo was for the best, so we continued, until she passed away this year.'

'And now you're writing under your own name?'

'Not exactly. The book I'm working on now will be in my name but I was halfway through a book when Gran passed away. I said we should cancel it and I'd repay the advance. Bryony persuaded me we should continue because Gran's fans were expecting that book. I agreed, and we did. Her fans would believe the book was written by Gran before she died. I was okay with that, all things considered and of course, I was dating Bryony at the time so I didn't really think about it as much as perhaps I should have. Then a few months ago, Bryony asked me to continue writing the books and we would say that I had found several 'lost' manuscripts of Gran's. That didn't seem right on many levels and I said no. We argued about it constantly and that's when I realised I had to stop seeing her, personally at least. That was two months ago but she's still trying to get me to agree.'

'And Hollywood? What did she mean about that?'

'She's negotiated movie rights on several of the books but they want me to go to Los Angeles and co-write the screenplays. I said I didn't think I wanted to do that. It's a lot of money and Bryony wants her cut which would be pretty substantial if the deal went ahead. I'm the Executor of Gran's estate and my sister and I are the only beneficiaries. Annabelle, my sister, will go along with whatever I want, as far as the books are concerned. Bryony keeps threatening to go to the tabloids and tell them that Gran hadn't written a word for many years. That wouldn't matter, I don't suppose, except to me. These 'revelations' soon blow over. But her fans might think Gran had let them down or betrayed them in some way and I don't want to do that to them or to Gran's memory... but enough's enough. Bryony will either do it or she won't. I can't keep fighting with her. My lawyers are terminating the contracts today. There'll be some legal issues to resolve but they can sort that out. That's it. End of story.'

Gabriel waited while Holly processed what he'd told her.

'I'm so sorry, Gabriel. It's put you in a difficult position. But I don't think your grandmother's fans would feel betrayed. If you told them what you've just told me, I think they'll see that she trusted you to write her books the way she would have written them, or the way she wanted them to be written. And women don't have a problem with men writing romance.'

'Really?' Gabriel looked into Holly's eyes. 'I can ask one fan right now. My grandmother was Gabriella Mann. I wrote the book you're currently reading. The book you were hiding from Ivy behind the cushion of your kitchen

166

armchair.'

Chapter Thirty-One

Wednesday, 23rd December

'Gabriella Mann!' Ivy spat out her early morning coffee, she was laughing so hard. 'Gabriel Hardwick, that hunk of a man next door, the one who looks like a superhero even when he's hunched over his laptop and wearing his glasses – *he* is Gabriella Mann? I thought I'd heard everything but that takes the Christmas gingerbread biscuit. I think I'll call him Gaby from now on.'

Holly glowered at her. 'No you will not. Gabriella Mann was Gabriel's grandmother, remember. He loved her very much. Think how you'd feel if someone started making fun of Gramps' memory. It isn't funny and it isn't nice. Besides, it's not strictly public knowledge, so you mustn't tell anyone. Promise me, Ivy. I know everyone in this village loves to gossip including you and me but I draw the line at this. We're telling Mum and Gramps because they can both keep secrets, but at the moment no one else must know.'

Ivy's shoulders shook. 'Okay, okay. I'll try. But when it's just us, please let me make fun of him. Please, please, pretty please. Just a little bit.'

'No. I mean it, Ivy. No. Or I'll start spreading tales about you and Ned Stelling.'

Ivy stopped laughing and narrowed her eyes.

'What makes you think there's anything to tell?'

'Because there's something going on between you two and even though I'm not sure what it is, if you start talking about Gabriel being Gabriella Mann, I'll start making

168

things up about you and Ned.'

'Threats, eh? Are you taking a leaf out of Bryony's book? It's unlike you to do something like that. You must've really fallen for Gabriella, sorry, Gabriel.' She grinned over the rim of her coffee mug. 'And you haven't told me what happened after Gabriel came out of the closet, so to speak. Did you act out one of those passionate sex scenes from the books? Is it, 'his books', or 'her books', now we know that Gabriel writes them? And was it like, "now let's turn to page 69 and act out this scene"?'

'Ho, Ho, Ho. Aren't you funny this morning? But I want to be serious for a moment. Can you do that? Or are you going to make fun of what I'm going to say?'

Ivy helped herself to a mince pie and held it in front of her mouth, placing her other hand on her heart and fluttering her eyelashes.

'Oh mince pie, I love you. Oh Ivy, I love you too. We were meant to be together. Bite me, bite me.' She bit into the pastry, making oh and ah sounds as she did.

'I think that answers my question,' Holly said, turning away to make herself more coffee.

'Oh don't be such a grouch. I'm sorry, but it's funny. At least I think it's funny. Okay. I'll be serious. What do you want to tell me?'

Holly turned and leant against the worktop. She tipped her head to one side and looked at her sister. Could she rely on her to take this seriously? Ivy loved to see the funny side of everything, but she could be serious when the situation called for it. She'd risk it.

'When Gabriel told me last night, I was really surprised, in spite of everything I'd just said to him. He asked me how I felt about it. I told him that whilst it didn't bother me, as a fan of Gabriella Mann, to find out that a man had written those books, it felt a little odd for me as a person, to discover that *he* was that man. He asked me why and I said it was probably just the shock of it. That once it had sunk in, it wouldn't make any difference. But you're right about the sex scenes. I mean, yesterday evening I was wondering what Gabriel would be like in bed. Last night, all I kept telling myself was, Oh my God! He wrote that steamy sex scene in chapter twenty-five, or whatever. He writes sex scenes that have you blushing and wriggling in the chair, just reading them. Imagine him actually doing those things he writes about. Oh God! I'm getting turned on just thinking about it.'

Ivy grinned. 'So... That must mean that all you did last night *was* think about it. You didn't actually do anything? Did he try anything? Did he make any moves at all? Did he kiss you?'

Holly shook her head. 'No. Nothing. He didn't do a thing. After I'd said it wouldn't make any difference, he suddenly jumped up, said he had completely forgotten about supper and dashed out to the kitchen to check it was okay. It was, so we sat down and had supper and talked about everything except romance and romance authors. We mainly talked about Christmas and the snow. Stuff like that. Then I said I was tired and that I'd see him tomorrow. Being today, of course.'

'And he didn't kiss you good night?'

'No.'

'Did he ask you out? As in, "Now you know all about me, will you be my girlfriend?" Or at least, "Will you go on a date with me?" He didn't say anything like that?'

'No. I just said that I'd see him tomorrow. He walked me to the door. Our door. But he didn't stand under the mistletoe. He sort of, hung back. He said good night and that he'd see me tomorrow. That was it.'

'For a writer of steamy romances, the guy isn't very

bloody romantic... Or steamy. Is he?'

Holly shrugged. 'They say it's the quiet ones who are always the most passionate. But he has got a lot on his mind. It's been an eventful few days, to say the least. And we have only just met. Perhaps he wants to take things slowly.'

Ivy nodded. 'Perhaps he does. What have you done with that latest Gabriella Mann romance you were reading? I think I'd like to read it. It'll have a whole new meaning now I know who the author really is.'

Chapter Thirty-Two

Gabriel felt as if a heavy burden had been lifted from his shoulders. Despite Bryony's threats, he didn't think she would actually do anything. It wasn't in her interest. And she'd still get her commission on all the deals and books to date. She had been a good agent in most respects to both he and his grandmother, and whilst he was glad to be free of her by instructing his lawyers to terminate their contract, he was sad that their long business relationship had had to end this way.

But now he must look to the future, to his new book, to new opportunities and, he hoped more than anything else, to the start of a relationship with Holly Gilroy.

And to Christmas... of course. Tomorrow was Christmas Eve, which meant he only had today and tomorrow to do his Christmas shopping. He had better get a move on, especially as it was snowing again. Heavily. It was coming down so thick and fast that he couldn't see further than a few feet in front of him. It was virtually a white-out.

Last night had been bitterly cold when he had walked Holly to her door and icicles hung beside the mistletoe that he had tried to avoid. Not because he didn't want to kiss Holly. He did. Very much so. But because he got the distinct impression that she was feeling nervous. Apprehensive even. And she hadn't been like that the night she'd reached up and kissed him. He had wanted to ask her out, but it was better to let the news he had told her, sink in overnight.

This morning wasn't quite as cold as last night and

although he couldn't see them through the curtain of thick, white flakes, he could hear the screams of delight and gurgles of laughter from Lulu and Sean, Tabby and Robin's children from the cottage next door. They must be playing in the snow. Probably building a snowman, or throwing snowballs at one another. Beryl and Bill's dog, Bonnie, must also be outside if the barks echoing in the morning air were anything to go by.

He smiled. It was early. Not quite eight o'clock. The shops weren't open yet. He should be working on his book. But that could wait. It was Christmas, after all. He would head outside. He grabbed his coat and pulled on his boots, remembering to retrieve his gloves from the kitchen chair where he had left them last night.

'Having fun?' he asked when Lulu came bounding towards him, followed by Sean, a few inches behind her and Bonnie, who was clearly so excited that she careered into Sean, knocking him into Lulu. All three of them ended up in a cloud of snow at Gabriel's feet, resulting in Lulu and Sean bursting into tears. Bonnie scrambled to her paws, wagged her tail and licked their faces for all she was worth.

'You're okay,' Gabriel said, lifting each child in each of his arms and spinning round with them until they forgot what they were crying about and gurgled with laughter once more. Bonnie ran in circles round and round Gabriel's legs.

'Good morning.'

Gabriel stopped spinning the moment he heard Holly's voice.

'Good morning to you,' he said. 'Want to join us?'

'Not spinning, no. Thanks all the same.'

Gabriel set the children down on the ground and they charged around with Bonnie chasing after them.

'Life is so simple when you're young,' he said.

173

'It can be simple when you're older. It's not your age that matters. It's what's in your heart that counts. Or so Gramps always says.'

'Help us build a snowman. Help us build a snowman. Help us build a snowman.' Lulu and Sean tugged at Gabriel's coat.

Gabriel laughed. 'Why ask once when you can ask three times. Only if you ask Holly to help us too.'

Holly shook her head but the children had taken the bait.

'Help us build a snowman. Help us build a snowman. Help us build a snowman.'

'Okay. I'll help. But you've got to go to Holly Cottage first. That's the cottage over there and get Ivy to come and help as well.'

Sean looked concerned. 'Why does Ivy live in Holly Cottage if her name is Ivy? Shouldn't she live in Ivy Cottage?'

'You're right, she should. And sometimes I really wish she did,' Holly added quietly. 'But she's staying with me in my cottage. Run along and get her and then we'll all help build a snowman.'

The children ran off in shrieks of laughter to bring Ivy out to play. And Bonnie wasn't far behind.

'Why are you looking at me like that?' Gabriel asked.

Holly smiled. 'For someone who doesn't like children or dogs, I think you're in the wrong place.'

He smiled back. 'I told you, it's only the ones who won't stop barking that I don't like, and as for the dog...' He winked at her.

'I think we have a toboggan somewhere. It's probably in the loft. Perhaps the children would like to go tobogganing. There's a long slope just over there, flattening out for fifty feet or so, before sloping down again into the village. As long as they stayed on the top slope and were able to stop on the flat, they'll be perfectly safe and they'll have a lot of fun. Ivy and I did it every time it snowed when we were young. And there's so much snow around that even if they fall off, they won't get hurt. Although they are quite young, so perhaps one of us should go down with them.'

'Shall I go and get it?' Gabriel asked.

'Yes, please. Ask Ivy to let you in and tell her what you're looking for. I'll go and ask Tabby and Robin if it's okay.'

Gabriel made his way to Holly Cottage and although it was only a walk of less than five minutes from where he had been standing to Holly's front door, when Ivy saw him she burst out laughing.

'You look like an abominable snowman. You're covered from head to toe in snow.'

'Good morning, Ivy,' Gabriel said. 'Is that what it is? And I thought it was raining. Holly has sent me to look for a toboggan. Grrr.'

He pulled a face and raising his arms up in the air, ran towards the children pretending to be a yeti. They screamed and ran, with Bonnie chasing after them.

'You're clearly not a morning person,' Ivy said, acknowledging his monster impression. 'Holly looks like that first thing before she's had her coffee. Come in. I expect the toboggan's in the loft. Do you need a hand?'

He shook his head. 'No I'm fine. I think I saw it when we were getting the decorations down. I'll only be a few minutes. Don't you have children waiting for you to help build a snowman?' He laughed and headed towards the loft.

'Yes. I must thank Holly for that. I thought you didn't like children. Or dogs.'

He stopped at the top of the stairs and turned to face her. 'Like Scrooge, it seems I've woken up, a changed man. And with two days to spare. It didn't even take three spirits to show me the error of my ways. Just one. The Christmas spirit.'

He pulled down the loft ladder and climbed up.

'Ah. How sweet,' Ivy said.

When he came back down moments later, toboggan in hand, she was still hovering in the doorway but at least she had her coat and gloves on.

'Speaking of changed men,' she said. 'Holly told me that you write romance novels.'

'I do. Or at least I did. Now I'm writing a thriller.'

'Isn't romance thrilling?'

'Very much so. But I'm sure Holly also told you the reason why.'

'She did. What she didn't tell me, is when you two are going on a date. I mean an official date, as opposed to just wandering around together.'

He smiled at her. 'Perhaps we should go on a double date. Me and Holly, you and Ned. Don't look so surprised.'

'Holly told you?'

'No. It's obvious there's something going on between the two of you. In fact, I think I was the one who told Holly.'

'That's the thing I don't like about this village. Everyone knows everyone else's business. We were trying to keep it secret.'

'Why? You're both young, free and single. His mum and yours seem to get on very well, so there's no family feud to stop you from seeing one another. And it's not because your positions in life are unequal. Those days are long gone even in a village like this.' Gabriel shook his head and laughed. 'Sorry, that's the romance writer coming out in me. Always looking for a plot line.'

Ivy grinned. 'It's just that Ned and I, much like Holly and Paul, grew up together. We've known each other all our lives. We've been friends for as long as we can remember. We have coffee together when I'm here, the way friends do. Then suddenly the other day, I'm working in the pub and in he walks with that lopsided grin on his face, and wham! I'm not seeing him as Ned Stelling, the boy who used to push me in the pond, or the man who helps me carry my bags, or shares a coffee and a friendly chat. Or even as the local blacksmith. I'm seeing him as Ned Stelling, the hottest hunk in the village. Well, in our age bracket anyway.'

'And what's wrong with that?'

'Nothing's wrong with that. In fact, it's perfect. Too damn perfect. That's the problem.'

Gabriel shook his head. 'You've lost me, Ivy. What's the problem?'

'Why now? Why after all these years and all the times that Ned has walked in and out of The Snowdrop Inn, have I suddenly decided that he's the best thing since sliced bread? It makes no sense. That's why I wanted to keep it quiet. The minute people know, it's going to be: 'Ivy and Ned, Ned and Ivy. We always knew they'd end up together'. And what if we don't? I mean, what if this is just one of those spur of the moment things? Or the spirit of Christmas making us both do things we wouldn't normally do? What if it doesn't work out? I don't want to ruin our friendship. It'll be difficult enough coming back here with just him and me knowing what happened between us. We don't want everyone else talking about it and rubbing salt into our wounds. It's Holly and Paul all over again.'

'Firstly Ivy, love rarely makes sense.'

'Love! I didn't say anything about love.'

'You didn't have to. It's written all over your face when you talk about him. Secondly, it's nothing like Holly and Paul. They dated for a long time but discovered they were

177

really only friends. You and Ned have been friends for a long time and have recently discovered you want to be more. And thirdly, no one ever knows if things will work out when they start a relationship. It's a chance we all have to take. Love is worth the risk. Stop worrying about it and enjoy it. That's what romance is all about. Trust me, I'm a romance writer.' He winked at her.

'You're right. We should just bite the bullet and tell everyone we've started dating. But I do wish you'd stop using the word love. That terrifies the life out of me.'

'Love terrifies the life out of everyone at times. For a four letter word, it's pretty powerful stuff. Now I believe we have snowmen and women to build. And hills to slide down. We mustn't keep the children waiting.'

Ivy held the door open and let him walk through so that she could shut it behind him.

'And that's another thing that terrifies me,' she said, a worried look on her face. 'The thought of having children. Of having to bring up kids.'

'You and me both,' Gabriel said. 'But this'll be good practice.'

'Yeah. And with my luck, there'll probably be some broken bones.'

Chapter Thirty-Three

The morning had been much more fun than Ivy had expected. When Lulu and Sean had arrived at the door saying Holly had sent them to get her, to help them build a snowman, she was tempted to wring Holly's neck. But talking to Gabriel about her and Ned and then spending more than two hours frolicking in the snow with two kids, a manic dog and several adults – Tabby and Robin, Beryl and Bill, having all come out to join them – had made her put things in perspective. She had always said life should be lived to the full. So why was she trying to hide from it?

After showering again, following her exertions in the snow, she put on her favourite trousers and the jumper that Ned had told her "brought out the colour of her green eyes", and headed down to the village and Ned's smithy.

In spite of the cold outside, Ned, as usual was wearing only a T-shirt and jeans beneath his protective, leather apron. Ivy stood in the doorway and watched him as he held the latest workpiece over his anvil with a pair of tongs in one hand and a hammer with which to beat the heated metal, in the other. His muscles rippled and hardened with each resounding boom of the hammer strike and Ivy's heart thumped against her chest in time to his skilled movements. She had no idea what this current workpiece would turn out to be but everything Ned worked on became a piece of art – from an iron latch to an ornate gate or metal sculpture. He brought out the beauty in anything he touched.

And that included her.

She hadn't intended to jump into bed with him until they

had dated several times. They had agreed to take things slowly. Their new-found attraction had come as a surprise to both of them, thankfully at almost the same time, although Ned had told her that secretly, he had been a little in love with her for years. She definitely hadn't intended to jump into bed with him during daylight hours. But the day after Bryony's arrival, she'd come to tell him about the latest development in Holly's troubled love life, and he had been standing exactly as he was now.

She hadn't been able to stop herself.

Neither had he.

As she had marched decisively towards him, he had looked up, met her eyes and discarded his tools in time to sweep her up into his arms.

The heat she had felt when he had kissed her would have melted metal three times as fast as his forge. Passion blazed between them and before either of them had time to think, they had kissed their way upstairs and tumbled onto Ned's bed, leaving a trail of tossed clothes behind them. Ned hadn't even covered his forge or closed the doors of his smithy. Something he had only realised after half an hour of them making passionate love.

As they had lain, arms still wrapped tightly around one another, both in an almost trance-like state of 'after sex' ecstasy, Ned had suddenly jumped up, said, 'The forge!' and run downstairs. Ten minutes later, he had returned with two glasses of water and the biggest smile on his face.

'I've locked up,' he had said. 'And I thought you might be needing to quench your thirst. I know that I do. I also know I'd like to spend at least the next two hours in bed with you, unless you have other plans.'

Ivy had shaken her head and smiled. 'The only plans I have are my plans of what I intend to do with you. And it's only my thirst for your body that needs quenching.

Although on second thoughts, I might also need a quick glass of water.'

The way he had looked at her made her feel as if she were the most beautiful woman on earth.

Now, as she stood in the doorway watching him, he glanced up. The lines of concentration on his face disappeared, replaced instead by the sexiest smile Ivy had ever seen and eyes aflame with desire.

'How long have you been standing there?' he asked, putting his tools carefully to one side.

'Not long,' she said. 'I was admiring the view.'

'Have you come to just look, or is there something you're particularly interested in?'

He moved towards her and sparks of excitement flared into longing.

'There is one thing that's really taken my fancy. I saw it the other day and I can't stop thinking about it. I was wondering if I might take another look.'

'As it happens,' he said, taking her in his arms, 'I was just closing for an early lunch. A long, long lunch.'

'I'm quite hungry… as it happens,' she said, wrapping her arms around him. 'May I join you?'

He leant in to kiss her but she stopped him.

'I don't want to keep us secret, Ned. Whatever this is between us, and whatever happens, I want people to know that we're together. Especially as it's Christmas. I want to spend this Christmas with you as your girlfriend and I want the village to know that's what I am. Unless… unless you'd rather they didn't.'

His arms tightened around her. 'I've already told my mum. I know we said we wouldn't but I couldn't help it. I was fit to burst with happiness. I couldn't keep it in. I want to shout it from the rooftops, Ivy. I want to stand in the middle of The Snowdrop Inn and tell everyone at the top of my lungs that I love you.'

Ivy blinked several times. 'You... You love me?'

'I love you, Ivy Gilroy. Is that a problem? Because if it is, there's nothing I can do about it. I can't change the way I feel. And I can't pretend I don't feel it. I love you.'

Ivy shook her head and beamed at him. 'That's not a problem, Ned. Or if it is, I've got the same problem. Because, Ned Stelling, I love you too. Although I think I've only just realised it. But... I'd rather you didn't stand in the middle of The Snowdrop Inn and tell everyone how you feel. I think there have been more than enough people doing that in Mum's pub recently, don't you? Now kiss me please, Ned. We haven't got all day.'

Chapter Thirty-Four

Thursday, 24th December – Christmas Eve

'It's Christmas Eve!' Holly pulled back the kitchen curtains and peered out through her window. 'And it's *still* snowing. Ivy! Did you hear me?'

Ivy was leaning her elbows on the kitchen table, cradling a mug of coffee.

'The elves in Santa's workshop at the North Pole can hear you. I know it's Christmas Eve and I know it's still snowing, having just driven back here this morning from Ned's. That hill's getting harder to drive up. At this rate the village will be cut off again, like it was in Gramps' day and we'll all be snowed in.'

'I don't mind if we are. I don't mind if it snows and snows and snows until July at least. Then Gabriel won't be able to leave at the end of the holidays.'

'I don't think Gabriel *wants* to leave. I don't think you'll need snow to keep him here. I don't know if I should say this, but I heard him ask Mum whether she might be prepared to let him stay on after the New Year.'

'What? When?'

'Yesterday. When you were doing your last minute Christmas shopping. I popped in for a bite to eat at around three o'clock, having missed lunch. Gabriel was there and he was talking to Mum. I happened to hear what he said. Not that I was eavesdropping or anything.'

'No, of course. You wouldn't do that. So what did he say?'

'I only heard that bit. He said that he would like to stay on for a while and asked if Mum would be willing to let him rent Ivy Cottage on a weekly or monthly basis. He said he didn't care what it cost. She could name her price. Mum said he might regret that last part but yes, she would be happy to, even though the cottages are normally closed after New Year for maintenance and such like. She told him she likes to make sure they're ready to reopen in time for the Easter holidays.'

'So… he said he'd stay until Easter? He didn't mention it to me when he came into the pub last night. Or when he brought me home.'

'No. Mum said he *could* stay until Easter but that she had bookings for the cottage from Easter onwards. I didn't hear anything else, if anything else was said because Meg Stanbridge came in, shouting that one of the Gaggle Gang was missing and yelling that an outsider must have stolen it because no one in the village would be cruel enough to think they could cook one of her geese for Christmas dinner.'

'Oh my God, Ivy! Why didn't you tell me about this earlier?'

'Which part? The bit about Gabriel staying? Or the goose disappearing?'

Holly had to think about that for a second.

'Gabriel staying but then you should've instantly told me about the goose straight after. Has it been found? Why aren't we all out looking for it? Last time one of them went missing, the whole village formed a search party. We spent hours looking for it until we eventually discovered that someone had accidentally shut it in Meg's disused, outside loo, which for some reason, was the last place anyone thought of looking. Have they checked Meg's loo?'

Ivy giggled. 'I'm sure that's the first place some unlucky

person got to look. But don't panic. The goose is safe and sound. The Gaggle Gang are reunited and will be strutting their stuff at a venue near you in the not too distant future. It was the same goose that got locked in the loo, so we're all thinking that one's got an even more rebellious streak than the rest of them. This time it had gone into Meg's house and got itself shut in the larder. Apparently, it made quite a mess but it's none the worse for its adventure.'

'That's a relief. It means they'll be parading around the village as usual this afternoon, wearing their Christmas bows around their long, white necks. I love seeing that. Although in all this snow it might be difficult for them to get around. Only their orange beaks and heads may be visible. They'll look like little periscopes poking up from beneath the sea of white.'

Holly giggled as she saw that picture in her mind's eye.

'Henry's already thought of that. He said he'll drive them around the village in the trailer on the back of his tractor, so that everyone can see them, along with the presents to go under the tree of The Snowdrop Inn for The Snowdrop Bash.'

'This is going to be the best Christmas ever. I can feel it.'

'Yes. The one you'll tell your great-great-granddaughters about in years to come. Although I seem to remember the last time we had this conversation you felt very differently.'

Holly smiled. 'What can I say? Sometimes a few days can make all the difference. Life is very strange and it's always full of surprises.'

'Which is what I'm hoping my Christmas stocking will be this year. Full of surprises, not very strange. So... did anything happen between you and Gabriel last night after he brought you home?'

185

'No. Just as we got to the door, his phone rang. It was his sister calling from Hawaii. She'd forgotten the time difference and it was lunchtime there, around one-thirty. He said he'd call her back but I said he should talk to her and I was tired anyway, so I'd see him in the morning.'

'Idiot.'

'I know. I considered knocking on his door later but it was freezing cold and snowing and... well... I didn't want to seem too keen.'

'Or desperate. Oh well. There's always tonight. Speaking of which, we'd better get ourselves organised. Mum's got a long, long list of things she wants us to do.'

Chapter Thirty-Five

The Snowdrop Inn wouldn't look out of place in a fairy tale. Standing on its raised bank, covered in a thick layer of snow, it looked magical with multi-coloured fairy lights casting dancing shadows like sugarplum fairies all around. Icicles hung, like crystal Christmas decorations, from the bare boughs of the chestnut tree and to the left of it, the pond, still frozen solid, reflected the lights surrounding it on its mirror-like surface.

It had finally stopped snowing and the heavy clouds had drifted away to leave a sky full of twinkling stars and a moon, like a Christmas bauble of the gods, shone down, lighting a path across the still frozen Market Field to the door of The Snowdrop Inn.

Inside the pub, the two log fires roared and, together with the heat generated by the mass of partygoers, the place was hotter than Hell's kitchen. To an onlooker, it probably resembled Hell's kitchen although the occupants were having far too much fun for it to be Hell. Tables groaned under the weight of party food – including several batches of The Best Mince Pies in Hideaway Down – and drinks were flowing. People were singing and dancing as Christmas carols boomed out along with happy laughter, merry voices and the exchange of joyous seasonal greetings.

Petunia and Bartram and Ivy and Ned were particularly joyful, this being the first Snowdrop Bash they'd attended with their new partners. So were Holly and Gabriel although they'd popped outside for a moment to get a breath of the cold, night air to cool themselves down after dancing for several hours.

'Gran would have loved it here,' Gabriel said, his arm wrapped tightly around Holly's waist as they watched the partygoers through the frosted glass. 'I certainly do. I wish I'd found this place sooner.'

'Things might not have been the same if you had,' Holly said, looking up into his eyes. 'Timing is everything, Gramps always says. He also says that life gives us what we need, not necessarily what we ask for or what we think we want.'

'Life has given me what I asked for, what I need and what I want,' Gabriel replied. 'Or perhaps it was Santa because I asked him for it too.'

'Oh. And what did you ask Santa for?'

'I asked him for you, Holly. You're what I need and you're definitely what I want.'

She smiled up at him.

'Then Santa got a 'Buy one, get one free' kind of deal because I asked Santa for you. Well, what I actually asked him for, was for a chance to get to know you better. He's certainly delivered on that.'

'I'd say he's delivered on all counts. We even got our white Christmas. And I get to spend Christmas Day with you.'

'You are prepared for your first Christmas Day with the Gilroys, aren't you? It's going to be a long one. We start with champagne, and smoked salmon bagels. We open some presents and then we open the pub for two hours. After that, we have lunch. Mum always buys a turkey from Bartram that's big enough to feed fifteen people, so it'll be good to have some extra guests to help eat it. Then we go for a long walk and Gramps has already told me we're going to Hideaway Hole so that you and he can do a spot of fishing – even though the lake may possibly be frozen.'

'That sounds like fun.'

'Hmm. I'm not so sure. We'll come back here and sit by the fire playing charades or board games and Ivy will cheat. She always does. We'll open more presents and then we'll roast chestnuts and marshmallows and drink hot chocolate laced with brandy. Gramps will fall asleep and wake up in time for Christmas tea, which means more mince pies and Christmas cake. Oh, and Christmas crackers and silly hats. Mistletoe will chase Merlot and cause chaos and Mum will drink too much Baileys. Then we'll open the pub again for Christmas night. It gets pretty packed.'

'I'm looking forward to it,' Gabriel said. 'But not as much as I'm looking forward to opening my presents with you.'

'Well, as it's now past midnight it's officially Christmas Day. Perhaps I should tie myself up in a red bow and sit at the foot of your bed. I'd like to be the first Christmas present you wake up to on Christmas morning, if that's what you want.'

Gabriel pulled her closer to him.

'I certainly would, Holly. You have no idea how much I would. You've been the top of my Christmas list since the moment we first met. But I don't want you to be just my Christmas present. I want you to be my Christmas future too.'

He kissed her slowly, deeply, passionately, as if he would never stop kissing her.

But eventually he did.

'I've asked your mum if I can stay on at Ivy Cottage indefinitely,' he said, his voice heavy with desire. 'She said that I could stay until Easter, but she has bookings after that.'

'What will you do at Easter? Where will you go then?

189

Home? Although I suppose it's too soon to think about that and we can obviously work something out.'

'I don't think it's too soon to think about that and I know we can work something out. I'm hoping I won't be moving very far. Not very far at all. In fact, I'm hoping there's a chance I'll be able to move next door. The woman who lives there makes the best mince pies in Hideaway Down and I'm hoping that next Christmas we'll be making them together.'

Holly looked deep into his eyes.

'I think we can safely say that there is a very good chance of that,' she said. 'A very good chance indeed. She also likes to curl up in bed with her favourite book. She'd much rather curl up in bed with her favourite author, now that she knows who that author really is.'

Gabriel kissed her again.

'I know this is The Snowdrop Bash and I suppose we should really stay but I can't wait to open my first present. Is there any chance that we could go home and do that? And then, I've got some presents for you to open.'

Holly smiled.

'I've got some more presents for you, too. The entire village is here, so I'm sure we won't be missed. And if we are, I've a pretty good idea they'll know where we've gone. Besides, we'll be back here first thing tomorrow, so I'm sure Mum and Gramps won't mind, and Ivy and Ned won't notice. Let's go home and have a private party of our own.'

'I like the sound of that.'

Holly grabbed him by the collar and kissed him.

'Merry Christmas, Gabriel.'

He pulled her close to him in a passionate embrace.

'Merry Christmas, Holly. I have a feeling this is going to be my best Christmas ever.'

'I have a feeling this will be the first of many.'

Arm in arm, they made their way up the long, steep hill to Gilroy's Happy Holiday Cottages, knowing that this holiday was going to be very, very happy indeed.

THE END

Christmas Message and Thanks, from Emily

Thank you so much for reading, *A Christmas Hideaway*. I love the anticipation and excitement of the festive season so I had great fun writing this book. I hope you had as much fun reading it. If you did, I would love it if you could leave a brief review. I love being an author and it's wonderful to hear from readers who enjoy my books – either by way of a review, a comment on social media, or an email. So please don't be shy. Let me know if you liked it. Reviews also help other readers to decide whether or not to try one of my books, so just a line or two may make all the difference. Thanks so much.

I'm really looking forward to Christmas and I'll be posting photos of Christmassy things, from now until the Big Day. Why not come and join me on social media?

I hope you're looking forward to the festive season too and I'd like to take this opportunity to wish you a marvellously, magical, Merry Christmas. But if you don't celebrate Christmas, then I wish you a Happy, Healthy and Peaceful time.

I'm off now to make mince pies and gingerbread reindeers, sip Champagne and knock-back the Baileys. I may be some time….

MERRY CHRISTMAS! HAPPY HOLIDAYS!
Love,

Emily xx

COMING SOON

Catch A Falling Star

A Hideaway Down Novel (Book 2)

Sometimes stars need help to shine.

Laurel French is happy – and why wouldn't she be? She's young, free and single; she owns The Coffee Hideaway, lives in the prettiest village in East Sussex and is surrounded by friends... even if some of them are a little eccentric. What more could she want? Love? No, not Laurel. Love is the last thing Laurel wants to think about... because it's unrequited. Ned Stelling is in love with someone else.

Jamie McDay is miserable. Hollywood has become a gilded cage. The paparazzi are snapping at his heels, and since he dumped his co-star girlfriend in a spectacularly stupid public display, he's been dropped from the Vampire series that made him a heart-throb, movie star. Visiting his friend, Gabriel Hardwick will cheer him up. Hideaway Down may be a bit 'twee' but local stunner, Ivy Gilroy could definitely put a permanent smile on Jamie's face. That's if he can persuade her to dump her boyfriend, Ned.

To see details of my other books, please go to the books page on my website or scan the QR code, below. http://www.emilyharvale.com/books.

***

Scan or tap the code above to see Emily's books on Amazon

To read about me, my books, my work in progress and competitions, freebies, or to contact me, pop over to my website http://www.emilyharvale.com. To be the first to hear about new releases and other news, you can subscribe to my Readers' Club newsletter via the 'Sign me up' box. Or why not come and say 'Hello' on Facebook, Twitter or Pinterest. Hope to chat with you soon.

15544462R00113

Printed in Great Britain
by Amazon